THE PRINCESS AND THE LUMBERJACK

Kingdom of Daes Duo - Book 1

H L MULLER

H. L. Muller is Australian, and this book is written in United Kingdom/Australian English.

Second Edition.

ISBN: 978-0-6488610-2-7

Cover design by: Avadal Designs

Editing: Jess Webeck

Publisher: H. L. Muller

DEDICATION

To my younger self, who never thought we would get here, we made it.
This one is for you.

GLOSSARY

There are a few words in this story that can be hard to pronounce. I wanted to give you an idea of how they sound to me.

Adaira = A-dare-a

Daes = Days

Ika = Eye-ka

Evalyn = Ever-lyn

Kryler = Cry-la

PROLOGUE

Princess Gertrude - Ten years old

"That is no way for a future Queen to behave, Gertrude," Evalyn admonished.

Why was it always such a crime to have fun? I was running around my playroom, giggling at Evalyn. If it was un-queen like to play in a playroom, why did I have one? Evalyn was my governess and had joined me the summer I turned seven. I don't know why Elizabeth, my last governess, left. I liked Elizabeth; she was always extra nice and let me go out to see Stormy whenever I wanted. As a Princess, I spent my time in classes and training to be a Queen. Most of my friends have been my books and my teddies. When we went out to balls or small parties, I wasn't allowed to play with the other children as *it's not how a Princess should behave*. With my restricted lifestyle and my duties, I was limited in how I could meet or make friends, and I barely knew anyone outside of my own Palace home. Elizabeth was one of my few real friends, before she left. I have Evalyn now, and we became fast friends.

Evalyn and Mother were always talking and plotting ways that I could start spending time in Prince Charming's Kingdom, *"to build your relationship with Prince Charming,"* Mother had said. I didn't see the point. Charming never liked playing with me, anyway. He was the same age as my brother Harrison and they were always playing together with Charming's brother Ambrose. Every day I wished that Charming had a sister, so I could have a friend too. I don't know why Mother and Evalyn bothered so much. Ever since I can remember, it had been planned for me to marry Prince Charming when I turned eighteen. Prince Charming lived in the Kingdom on our western border and was the eldest son of King Kryler and Queen Pomona. He was tall for his age and had slick black hair which he always had combed to perfection. Charming was next in line to the throne, and I was to be his Queen.

"What are we going to do today, Evalyn?" I asked her, "Can we go for a picnic and see Stormy?"

Evalyn allowed it and started dressing me to go outdoors and making preparations for the day. We had done this before and it felt like a routine now.

While we ate lunch, we spoke about everything. What I was reading, what I was interested in learning about this year, my teddies, and what awful things Harrison had been up to in the Palace. Our conversations were usually based around me and we didn't speak of Evalyn's life much.

Evalyn made me feel safe; I knew that I could trust her with all of my truths. She asked questions and always seemed interested in anything I had to say.

Bouncing in excitement, I exclaimed "I have to tell you Evalyn, I have a crush on that boy." I pointed him out to Evalyn as we watched him walking across the grounds.

She looked shocked, "Him?"

"Yes, I don't know his name, but he is always genuinely nice to me when I see him in the gardens. I think he helps his father with the trees and gardening. He has the loveliest sea green eyes." I said with a sigh. "Do you think that one day I'll get to properly meet him?"

"Hmm," Evalyn replied, then remained quiet, not giving anything away to my confession.

Evalyn cut our trip short, so we didn't go to see Stormy. After we finished our picnic, we walked in silence back to the Palace. Once we returned to my rooms, Evalyn left me alone and went to her room. I was a little saddened that she had not responded much to my crush on the green-eyed boy.

I *knew* that I was to marry Prince Charming, but he never saw me! I was always going to his Kingdom and doing so many things to get the chance to see him, and whenever I did, he was never interested in seeing me!

I knew I was a very lucky girl; I was a Princess and I had everything anyone could want. All the books I read are about girls who hope to become a Princess and get saved by a handsome Prince. It felt wrong to be ungrateful for something I had that everyone else wanted, but I couldn't help but feel something was missing from my life. The stories I read never mentioned how cruel Princes are, or how lonely a Kingdom full of people can be. Settling in my window seat, I looked out over the gardens. I couldn't see the green-eyed boy, so I opened one of my favourite books and found myself lost in the story.

Looking up as my clock chimed, I realised that a few hours had gone by and Evalyn had not returned. This was unusual for her. Normally she was glued to my side. I left my rooms to go and find her. Maybe she was unwell and would need someone to care for her? I could do that, she is my friend, and she was always caring for me when I was ill.

Evalyn wasn't in her room, I asked the maids and servants I saw around the Palace and no one knew where she was. Mother would know, I could go and ask her.

I was walking up the hallway to my Mother's sitting room when I heard raised voices. I never liked being around Mother when she was angry, so I waited in the hall to hear what they were saying. I didn't want her to get angry at me for interrupting.

I could hear her footsteps as she paced across the floor, "She likes the farm boy? That's disgusting. She is betrothed to marry a Prince, Evalyn. She cannot be having feelings for other boys. Imagine what would happen if Charming or his parents knew about this. Has she told anyone besides you?"

"No, Your Majesty. She entrusted it only to me. Other than me, she doesn't have any friends and would not have mentioned it to Harrison or the lady's maids."

"Good. We must handle this quickly..." Mother's voice faded away, as I turned and walked away.

I could feel my heart breaking. Evalyn had gone to my mother and told her everything. How long had she been reporting to her? I couldn't stay to hear what they were going to do to 'handle' this situation. I ran through the halls, throwing myself through doorways and crashing into my bedroom. No one had stopped or followed me as I tore past them.

I didn't see Evalyn again until dinner with my family. Mother barely looked in my direction. This was a familiar tactic of hers, whenever she was displeased or upset with you, she would ignore you until she deemed it enough time before acknowledging you again. She didn't speak to me directly throughout dinner, only to Evalyn. I wondered that if I hadn't heard Evalyn talking to her, would I be trying to figure out what was wrong? I was turning it over in my mind, replaying all my conversations with Evalyn, trying to figure out what else she had told my Mother, when I heard my Father speak.

"That farm boy and his father have been dismissed as you requested, Cynthia." He spoke plainly to my mother, his voice conveying no emotion or remorse at losing two staff members, as if they and this conversation were of no consequence to him. Father turned back to Harrison and continued on his conversation, not noticing the crestfallen expression on my face. Mother and Evalyn were ignoring me too. A pit opened where my stomach used to be, churning full of guilt and anger. Who were they to think they could just ruin a family's life, because of me? I managed to excuse myself and rush back to my room. It was my fault. *If I hadn't felt this way about him, if I hadn't told Evalyn, this would have never happened.* I resolved myself to never confide in Evalyn, or anyone else, again. I would not let them hurt others to manipulate me.

It was all my fault.

Chapter One

PRINCESS GERTRUDE

*P*resent Day

I bolted upright, panting and on the verge of tears. Normally, I wake up to the sound of chirping birds outside and sunshine glimmering on my face. It had been a while since I had dreamed of that day with Evalyn. I shiver as I try to shake the emotions that that dream always brought on.

Today is my eighteenth birthday. Only one week until we officially announce our engagement at Prince Charming's twenty-first birthday ball, and two weeks until we will be married, settled and living in Prince Charming's Castle. I have been counting down to this all my life, and now there are only fourteen days left. One might imagine that I am excited to be married as I am in love and going to wed my soulmate, or that I am eager to fulfil my purpose and duty as Princess in marrying for the alliance it would ensure for my Kingdom. They would not expect the real reason behind my excitement is the need to be away from this Palace.

It has been hard living with Mother and Evalyn since that day, not that it had been easy before then. Over the last eight years I have isolated myself, keeping my thoughts and emotions private. No one in the Palace can be trusted. After the incident with Evalyn and the farm boy, I realised that everyone who lives in the Palace is owned by Mother and Father. All the servants and members of the court answer to them. If it ensured their favour with my Mother and Father, you could place bets on how soon they would betray me. It was a game I had started playing with myself, counting how long it would take.

I didn't allow anyone to see who the real Trudy is. Not even my brother Harrison. Harrison is three years older than me and at twenty-one, he is too busy trying to find a bride who can put up with him, and that Mother and Father approve of, to care about me. From the looks of things, no woman was up to the task.

It struck me as strange, not for the first time, that Mother and Father were so set on my marriage. They had arranged it from the moment I was born, yet never arranged anything for Harrison. I had spent many hours speculating whether they believed Harrison would easily be married, or wouldn't follow their orders anyway, and why they had prioritised my marriage over Harrison's. The only conclusion I can come to is that they believe he should choose his own Queen.

When Harrison turned twenty-one three months ago, there was a large celebration that lasted several days. The whole Kingdom rejoiced and celebrated their future King's coming of age. A similar celebration happened for his eighteenth birthday. Harrison was showered with gifts from noblemen and their ladies, from this Kingdom and others.

My birthday often went by unnoticed. I doubted the Kingdom remembered my birthday, from what little of the Kingdom I have seen. Evalyn had once told me that the market-place near the Palace had sales and special gifts that they gave each other to celebrate my birthday, but I have never been allowed out to witness it take place. Mother and Father would usually acknowledge my birthday by leaving me alone all day then summoning me to celebrate with a fancy dinner, accompanied by Prince Charming and his family. I am expecting this year to be much of the same. I am feeling very celebratory this year, I was almost out. I am almost free; well, as free as I could ever be as a Queen. I held out hope that I would be able to make some decisions for myself. I will be head of a household and family. I may not be as completely free as our citizens are, but I will have more freedom than I have now.

Having squashed the memories from my dream, I rise out of bed and hop into a steaming hot shower. Standing in the shower long enough to let the heat seep into my bones and really wake me up for the day. Not long into my shower, I could hear my lady's maids moving around my bedroom. This was usual of them, going about making my bed and preparing clothing for me to wear today. I sighed, enjoying my peace while it lasted. When I was alone, I didn't need to pretend, that would end the moment I left my bathroom.

Resigning myself, I dried off from my shower and entered my dressing room. Without needing to be asked one of my maid's followed to assist me with my hair and dress for the day. I never address them by name, I have made all the servants believe that I have never learnt their names because they are beneath me. I know who they are, but I need to protect them and myself. I will not be misled and betrayed by someone again, and I couldn't handle the thought of another person being hurt to get to me. Every time I meet a new person, I debate letting them get to know the real me, the Trudy who lives beneath the Princess. Letting them see the rude and heartless Gertrude always wins. I have tried to convince myself I am heartless, that I have no feelings. I struggle with lying to myself though. No matter how hard I try to suppress it all, I still care. As a defence mechanism, I do not allow anyone to get close enough to know who I really am, and sometimes I forget who I am too. It is a lonely and exhausting existence. *Two more weeks.* I need to keep reminding myself it is almost over.

There were a few times when I was eleven where I let my true feelings show and spoke up to Evalyn, Mother and Father.

They dismissed me, shoved me aside and showed me with their actions and words that I was nothing to them. Well, that was a lie. I am a marriage to another Kingdom to ensure our alliance. After a few attempts, I gave in and became who they wanted me to be.

"What would you like to wear today, Your Highness?" The maid asked as she finished braiding my waist length chocolate brown hair straight down my back.

I don't know why she bothered asking me. I have many beautiful gowns that Mother and Evalyn have acquired for me, yet I don't like wearing fancy dresses daily. I don't like the extra attention it brings to me.

"That one," I indicated one of my usual daily gowns. The dress is floor length navy blue and comes down past my elbows, with a scoop neckline. It was as plain and as ordinary as a Princess could get, and I loved it. Mother hated it as it resembled the servants' dresses. When I was fifteen, she threw all my plain dresses out and told me I was only allowed to wear the fancy dresses she had bought. Instead, I wore nothing but my night clothes until she allowed my plain dresses to return; with the stipulation that any balls, parties or events I went to Evalyn or Mother had to approve my outfit. It was a compromise that I was willing to make to ensure that I could be comfortable while at home.

Dressed and presentable for the day, I set off through the Palace heading for the Gardens. As usual at this time of day, the hallways were deserted. Father and Harrison were probably in a state meeting, and Mother was likely still in bed. I spent as much time as I could out in the gardens, watching the clouds, speaking to the insects and small animals roaming around, reading and just enjoying not being disturbed by anyone.

The garden was a misleading name. It was a miniature forest, roughly one and a half acres of trees, pathways and garden beds. Every day I chose a new spot to discover. Originally, I started moving around the garden each day to prevent anyone from finding me. Now I spent my time exploring and learning new things about the garden. I could never get lost here as there were clear paths and signs every ten meters pointing you in the direction of the Palace, although I frequently lost myself within my own mind or whichever book I was reading.

Wandering out along the main paths, I relished the sound of autumn leaves crunching beneath my boots and the solitude of being alone in my gardens. There was a chill in the air, and it upsets me to think about Autumn ending. At least I will be in my new home for winter and will not have to deal with hours being trapped inside with Evalyn. I knew my peace would be short-lived today, and determined to enjoy it while I can, I walk to my favourite spot in the whole garden. It is a large old oak tree, with huge twisting roots that created a small seat. I sat and closed my eyes, listening to the sounds of nature around me. I fell into a light meditation until I heard footsteps approaching.

Looking around the garden it didn't surprise me to see one of the footmen approaching.

"Princess Gertrude," he paused and bowed when he was a few paces away, "Miss Evalyn would like to see you in your room."

Sighing, I rose and followed him back into the Palace. I am eighteen today and yet my governess is still ordering me around. *Two weeks, Trudy. You are here for two more weeks, then you are free from her forever.* My rooms were quite modest compared to Harrison's, Mother's and Father's, whose were much larger. I walked into my small sitting room that held my desk, bookcase couch and found Evalyn siting at the dining table. This room opened into my bedroom, the walls were a soft pink, my furniture made with a burgundy wood, and cream linens covered my bed, couch and sitting chair.

"Come Gertrude, you need to eat then start getting ready for our guests tonight." Evalyn motioned me towards my dining table.

For so long, I had been the submissive, quiet Princess. What

was two more weeks to keep the peace? It did not go unnoticed
that she did not rise when I entered the room, curtsy or address
me correctly. When we were alone, Evalyn never failed to show
me that she did not respect me. That I disgusted and disap-
pointed her in some way. When I was younger, I tried telling
Mother and Father. They either didn't care or didn't believe me.
In company Evalyn was a model lady, following all rules and
traditions.

Not playing into her manipulative game, I sat at the table
and began eating. The kitchen had sent up my favourite dish,
beef and vegetable stew with fluffy mashed potatoes. I smiled,
someone in the kitchens had likely remembered it was my
favourite and decided to give me what gift they could for my
birthday. Eating in silence was common for me, I ignored Evalyn
as she sat there watching me eat. I'm not sure what she was
hoping for, a reaction of some kind maybe. Half way though my
lunch, Evalyn stood and without another word left the room.
Perfectly timed as always, the moment the last spoonful entered
my mouth, my lady's maids entered the room.

"Evalyn has asked me to shower you and wash your hair, as
you had spent the morning in the gardens" the first maid
told me.

It was a dig I was expecting, Evalyn did not condone me
spending so much time outdoors alone since the farm boy incident. Even though I had showered this morning, I decided it
wasn't worth arguing. Evalyn would get her way in the end
anyway and refusing would only cause the lady's maids more
trouble than they needed. I left the dining table and took myself
to the shower, at least I could be alone in here. Washing out my
hair, I lost myself within my mind, thinking about all the 'what
ifs' that existed in my short life.

What if I wasn't a Princess?
What if I wasn't betrothed to Prince Charming?
What if I never told Evalyn about the green-eyed farm boy?
What if I was friends with the lady's maids?

What if I allowed Evalyn and Mother to corrupt and change me to be like them?

What if I was the real Trudy, and let my true self show?

What if Prince Charming was worse than Mother and Evalyn?

I was drawn out of my thoughts by a knock on the door and one of the maids went to answer it. Looking down I realised I was dried, dressed and styled for the evening. I was dressed in a soft aquamarine gown, styled to sit off my shoulders and with a sweetheart neckline. The dress had no beading or lace designs and was quite plain. The maids had dressed it up with a chunky yet jewelled necklace, and my hair was bound in a curly bun with a tiara sitting on top. I looked glamorous and elegant.

"That was the footman, Your Highness. We have fifteen minutes before your guests are due to arrive. The Queen would like you to be present for the welcome downstairs." The maid informed me as she re-entered my dressing room.

"Am I ready?" I asked with a sigh, looking over my appearance in the mirror again. After spraying me with a floral perfume, the maids deemed me ready and I walked into the hallway to the waiting footman.

Chapter Two

PRINCESS GERTRUDE

I joined Mother, Father and Harrison in the formal sitting room off the main entrance hall. This is where we met and greeted all our guests. I had hardly sat down when the footman announced the arrival of King Kryler and Prince Charming.

Charming had grown into an odd-looking man. I had heard him called handsome, but I had a feeling that had more to do with his title of *Crown Prince* than his actual appearance. He is pale and plain. As I was five feet tall, most people towered over me; at five foot two, Charming did not. He had been tall for his age at thirteen but hadn't grown since then. He is stick thin, with next to no muscle definition or strength. He has the body of a spoilt Prince, who has never had to work or do anything for himself in his life. Charming looked nothing like his younger brother Ambrose. He was what I liked to call a "typical knight" in all mannerisms and looks. Ambrose stood tall at 6 feet, and had the same black hair as his brother, yet it always looked wavy and windswept. He was tanned from spending too much time in the sun, and his muscles had muscles. I watched as Harrison looked around the room, probably searching for Ambrose.

Those two had formed a friendship after being separated from Charming and myself several times. Ambrose had always been kind and friendly to me, it would have been nice if he were here to celebrate my birthday too.

"Greetings, dear friends," King Kryler began speaking to my parents. "Sorry Ambrose could not make it tonight, he is off on another quest and would not quit it. You know how stubborn the boy can be."

My eyes were still on Harrison and I saw his shoulders sag and a flicker of disappointment and pain flash across his face, before smoothing back into his easy grin. I wonder what was behind that.

Evalyn had raised me to play the same role when I was in company. I was to be quiet, to speak only when directly asked a question and to follow Mother's orders. I was forgotten and pushed to the sidelines as a good Princess should be. Usually I enjoyed falling into the character created for me, it allowed me to keep my distance and avoid connecting with anyone. Today, I do not want to be quiet and forgotten. Walking directly to Charming, I injected myself into his conversation with Harrison.

"Good evening, Your Highness," I curtsied and looked up at him from under my eyelashes. We always spoke with proper titles, even after all these years of friendship.

"Good evening, Princess Gertrude. Hope you are well." Charming grumbled without turning to me. It was clear he didn't want to speak to me tonight. Harrison looked triumphant; probably delighted that he will have one more thing to tease me about.

"Yes, I am quite well, yourself?" I persevered.

Charming let out a heavy sigh and answered again without turning back to me. "Yes, I am excellent."

The door opened and the butler entered the room, cutting off my attempt at further conversation.

"Your Majesties, Your Highnesses, dinner is ready." The

butler bowed and held the door open as we fell into rank and walked into the dining room. Mother and Father entered first, followed by King Kryler, Harrison, Charming and myself last.

I would have thought that due to it being my birthday celebratory dinner, and having two weeks until our wedding, Mother would have sat Charming and I together. However, I was seated between King Kryler and Harrison.

Dinner was spent discussing trade and state affairs. I stopped paying attention around the entree and tuned back in when King Kryler asked me a question as dessert was being served.

"Gertrude, is there not to be a ball or any celebration for your upcoming birthday?"

Upcoming? It's today, surely you dingbats realise why you are here?

"This is all the celebration I require, Your Majesty." I looked down at the plate as it was placed in front of me and smiled softly. It held a large slice of chocolate sponge cake with a dollop of whipped cream, covered in melted chocolate and topped with a strawberry. Looking around the table, my smile grew noticing that everyone else had a vanilla cheesecake. They had remembered my birthday after all!

"Well, Charming is having a ball next weekend for his twenty-first birthday. I am sure we will all have a great time celebrating *his* birthday," King Kryler continued.

"And we must not forget about our announcement," Father added.

"Of course not," Charming replied, never looking in my direction.

Shortly after dessert, King Kryler and Prince Charming left, returning to their Castle. Usually, they would stay the night due to the long journey home.

I went to bed that night, disheartened and full of despair. No one had even said Happy Birthday to me. I received no gifts or acknowledgements, other than the cake for dessert, and my favourite lunch. I smiled at the thought of that huge slice of cake. Someone in the kitchens remembered and cared. I wanted to go and thank them. The thought of the admonishment I would receive from Evalyn stopped me. All I could do is cherish that slice of hope, knowing that someone remembered. That someone cared. Even if they thought of me as a cruel and heartless bitch.

Chapter Three

PRINCESS GERTRUDE

The week after my birthday passed quickly, and today was Prince Charming's twenty-first birthday. I was so excited for the ball tonight, even the storm clouds rolling in couldn't affect me. Our engagement will be announced tonight, then I only have one week to wait before we are married. The thought of marrying Prince Charming had been an abstract certainty all my life. I had known it would happen, ever since I could remember. Now that it was here, it was a little daunting. *Would Charming expect me to consummate the marriage with him straight away? Would he be gentle and caring or demanding and rough? Does Charming have experience with sex and women?*

After Charming's behaviour at dinner for my birthday, I knew that our relationship was going to be a lot of hard work, but I was willing to persevere to get away from this Palace. It was perplexing to think that our mothers had been planning this for eighteen years. Two years ago, Queen Pomona passed away, leaving King Kryler with his sons. King Kryler was growing ill and now seemed determined to ensure his throne was secured with Charming married and settled with an heir of his own. This match is beneficial for both Kingdoms, securing an ongoing alliance between us. In the centuries that the Kingdoms have coexisted there has not been a marriage between the two.

Unable to go outside due to the weather, I spent my morning reading and watching the rain, waiting for Evalyn and my lady's maids to attend me. I was lost staring out the window when I heard footsteps approaching and someone knocking at the door.

"Enter," I called out without moving, my eyes remained staring out at the rain, assuming it was Evalyn. It was rare for her, or a ladies' maid, to knock. They usually just let themselves in and did what they wanted, yet on occasion they would knock and seek my consent to enter.

"What a surprise. You are sitting around doing nothing." The rough clear voice of my brother Harrison broke through my revelry, whipping my head around to look at him.

"Harrison, what are you doing here?" Shocked and hesitant I rose to bow to Harrison. He may be my brother, but he is the Crown Prince. Harrison only sought me out to antagonise me, unless it was required, or he needed something.

"Can your brother not come in to wish you well on this magnificent day of yours?" the sarcasm in his voice was so thick, like I could reach out and touch it.

"Of course, you can," I turned my back to him, so he could not see my eyes roll. "Are you looking forward to the ball tonight? Hoping you can snare a fair maiden's attention? How is that wife hunt of yours going, brother dear?"

Harrison's eyes bulged, clearly annoyed with me or the notion of wife hunting. I smirked and batted my eyelashes over my shoulder, only setting him off further. He was a Prince though, with years' worth of political debates and war meeting training. He could manoeuvre any conversation easily. I think he forgot that I was also trained to handle political debates and was raised to be a Queen.

"Tell me, Gertrude, do you plan to show any emotion, despite hate, tonight? Plan on telling Charming that you are not capable of love? Or just skip straight to the consummation of the engagement and hope that will make you feel something?"

I had years of experience of dealing with Harrison when he behaved like this. I scoffed "Not capable of feeling love! Good one Harrison! How long did that take you to think up? Now, is there anything else I can help you with? If not, I have a ball to prepare for."

"It is noon. Need four hours to get ready, do you?" He scoffed, "It won't help your hideousness." He started laughing to himself as he walked out of my rooms, calling over his shoulder, "Don't forget to trim up if you plan on giving Charming any of the goods."

The lady's maids entered as Harrison left, and the next four hours were spent washing, drying, styling and dressing me for the ball. Often when it came to clothing for balls, I was not allowed any input in the design or choice in what I wore. However, as today was my engagement announcement, I had requested a specific dress that Mother and Evalyn had approved.

I was dressed in an elegant sea-green floor length ball gown with matching slippers. The ball gown had a high lace neckline, fitted tight across my torso, and held up with a small beaded button at the back of my neck. The dress was backless down to my waist and had cap sleeves with random sea glass beads placed across the shoulders and bodice. The gown then flared out into the skirt that trailed behind me as I walked. With the way the beading caught the light, I looked like I was shining. My waist length chocolate brown hair was unbound and styled in soft waves cascading down my back. I was not a vain person and did not believe that the world began and ended with good looks. However, I was not ashamed to think myself beautiful at times and believed this dress to capture and accentuate all the good features I possess.

I met Mother, Father and Harrison in the entrance hall. Father and Harrison were dressed in matching pale grey tailored suits, with sky blue dress shirts. Grey and sky blue were our family's colours and Father and Harrison usually wore this attire to formal events we attended. Father and Harrison both had long hair past their shoulders as in our family it was tradition for the men to have long hair. Father's greying chocolate brown hair was up in a ponytail while Harrison's was un-styled. Harrison and I got our colouring from Father. Mother wore a vibrant orange dress that washed out her features and, in my opinion, was too overpowering for her. Her pale blonde hair was styled in a large elegant bun, adorned with several colourful pins. We each wore a crown, showcasing our status to those that would be at the party tonight.

We were quiet as we all loaded into the carriage and travelled to the ball. The carriage ride was as quiet and peaceful as possible. I was not allowed to bring my book for the journey, as the last time I brought a book to a Ball I spent the entire time sulking. We had arrived at the Ball at the exact moment I got to the best part and wasn't allowed to pick up my book again for hours. With no book today, I spent my time watching our Kingdom as we travelled through it. I saw enormous forests on either side of the main road, and small villages popped up sporadically. Our carriage stopped briefly on the outskirts of a village called Adaira. We did not get out of the carriage, only waited long enough for the horses to be swapped for the rest of the journey. We would stop and swap them here again on our journey home.

Arriving at 8 o'clock the footmen helped us exit the carriage and I fell into line shadowing my family as we walked into the Castle that was soon to be my home. I had been here several times and it had never felt more welcoming than it did now.

Mother and Father were introduced to the ballroom first, followed by Harrison then me. We were always introduced in this order as they outranked me and took priority. The ballroom was large and extravagant, it had never looked this beautiful before. The room had over twenty chandeliers lighting the space. The gold grand staircase led down to a white marble floor, which tonight was full of women in colourful dresses and men in tuxedos or suits. The centre of the room was opened for when the dancing will commence, and along the right wall of the ballroom there were tables covered in food, drinks and delicacies from all over the Kingdom.

"Good evening, Your Majesties, Your Highnesses," Charming greeted us with a bow.

We all said hello then moved further into the ballroom, allowing him the time and space needed to continue welcoming the other arriving guests. Thrumming with excitement I could not stop myself from watching Charming. The line of arriving guests was dwindling and soon I would finally get my chance to open the ball, joining Prince Charming in the first dance.

Charming headed in my direction with a resigned look on his face, I lit up. *This is it!* Halfway across the room, Charming stopped in his tracks distracted by the entrance of a late guest. Unknown to me, she let herself into the ballroom, unaccompanied and not waiting to be announced. The whole room went quiet as we turn and watch her enter. This mystery woman was wearing a glittering and shimmering silver and golden ball gown, with clear glass slippers peeking out as she descends the staircase. Her blonde hair was up in a twisted bun, with a decorative black hair band, and she has captured the whole room with her beauty.

I stood there aghast as Prince Charming walked directly to this mystery woman, bows and starts conversing with her.

"It's okay. He needs to greet all his guests," Mother mutters to me. "Mason, do we know who she is? I cannot recognise her."

"I do not know who she is Cynthia. I have never seen her before." Father answered keeping his voice low.

"Me neither," Harrison added on.

"Find out. Now." Mother ordered in a whisper, sending Father and Harrison off into the crowded room.

NO! No! This could not be happening. Charming was dancing with this Mystery Woman. My mouth fell open in horror and fury. He is opening the ball with this woman? This is my right, my duty, and she just walked in and took it.

"What does this mean, Mother?" I ask under my breath. Careful of the ears that could be listening.

"I don't know, Gertrude. We will sort this mess out when your Father returns. We watch as Charming twists and turns her all over the dance floor. A heavy weight sags on my shoulders. That was meant to be me. Finishing the dance, Charming escorted her outside into his garden. I am tempted to interrupt them; I was raised better though. I know I could not make a scene in public.

What should I do? Should I follow him? I turn to Mother for guidance and as I open my mouth to speak, Father cuts me off as he re-joined us.

"No-one knows her name. King Kryler did not know that he was speaking to or interested in any other women. The King, like the idiot he is," Father spoke under his breath, "does not know what is going on, but the engagement announcement is to go ahead as planned once he returns from the garden with her." Father stated, looking between me and Mother.

"Prince Charming is in the garden with her?" Mother asks, her voice rising as she spoke, anger lacing her tone. I glance around the room, checking if we have any attention on us, and cannot see anyone staring. It is unusual for Mother to let her reactions show like this when we were amongst company. "He is probably just catching up with an old friend. I'm sure you have nothing to worry about. He is aware of the arrangement for him to marry you. Yes, we confirmed plans only the other day." She spoke like she was trying to convince herself, rather than me, of this and appeared to calm down.

I knew in my heart that my duty to my Kingdom always came first, and that included marrying Prince Charming. I believed that as a Prince, he would have the same sense of duty and honour.

"We will just need to wait until he returns from the gardens, dear." Father told Mother. Easing her stress further. It didn't calm me though.

For a few minutes, I remained in the same spot, watching and waiting for Prince Charming to return to the party. In an attempt to distract myself, I began to speak with other nobles from several Kingdoms who had travelled in for the ball. I dance with Father as custom and pick at the many luxurious foods placed on the edge of the ball room.

"Snubbed were you, Sister dear? Did you even get the chance to speak with him? What is to happen with you now?" Harrison spoke so low and close to my ear, I cannot handle him now, not on top of Charming's current whereabouts. Without acknowledging Harrison's questions, I turn and join another conversation.

The clock chiming midnight alerted me to how much time had passed. How could Charming still be outside with this woman? I glance around the room again and notice Harrison and Ambrose talking near the entrance to the gardens.

Through the doors behind them, it was not Charming who first re-entered the ballroom, it was the Mystery Woman. She tore across the dance floor, crashing into couples in her haste, launching up the stairs and running through the exit. Just like when she entered the ballroom at the beginning of the night, the whole room was startled by her sudden interruption. The music had cut off and everyone was still and silent as they watched her make her way through the room. As the Mystery Woman hit the top of the stairs, Prince Charming raced into the room chasing after her.

"Wait! Don't go!" Charming called out.

In a daze, I walk towards the staircase out of the ballroom. I follow them out to the entrance of the Castle, along with a handful of other people I was unable to focus on. When I step outside, I saw the King's guards chasing after a golden carriage, and Prince Charming standing there holding a single Glass Slipper.

Chapter Four

PRINCESS GERTRUDE

urning with an awestruck grin on his face, Charming's expression falls when he sees me. Without paying attention to the other guests standing around us, he bows slightly to me. "Ah, hello Princess Gertrude."

"Good evening, Prince Charming or I suppose I should say 'good morning' as it is now after midnight. Please tell me, who was that woman?" I keep my tone soft and civil, as I had been trained to.

"I don't know," he sounds dumbstruck. "I only met her tonight. You didn't happen to recognise her, did you? I didn't even get the chance to get her name! Oh, how foolish of me!"

He's not serious, is he? He had dismissed me for a woman that he didn't know? "Do you remember that we were to announce something at the ball tonight?" I ask, keeping my face and voice clear of emotion, aware of all the watching eyes and listening ears.

"Announcement? The only thing planned for tonight was my birthday celebration. I am so glad that everyone was able to make it. You included, even though we are not as close as one would expect." He replies dismissively, turning and walking back up the stairs and into the Castle.

I couldn't tell if he was completely oblivious and had forgotten about the engagement, or if he was trying to manipulate the situation, and pretending was not aware of it to get out of it.

"And what would they expect?" I ask him, following him into the Castle.

"What happened, son?" King Kryler asks briskly as we meet him in the entry foyer. "Who was that woman?"

"Oh father, I think I am in love!" Charming exclaims, his heart in his eyes as he claps his Father on the shoulder. "Have you ever seen a woman so beautiful and captivating? I have sent the Castle guards after her. As soon as she is found I will marry her and make her my Queen."

"Marry *her*?" Mother shrieked, as she and Father join us in the foyer.

"I was so caught up in her, I didn't even ask for her name. She lost her glass slipper though, and I will try it on every maiden in the land if I must. I will find my Mystery Princess." Charming continues, ignoring Mother's question. Disbelief pulses through me, squeezing down on my throat and preventing me from speaking. "I am unsure why she had to leave in such a hurry, she was speaking of pumpkins, mice and 'wonderful things'. I'm sure it will be quite the story when I hear it from her in full one day. She was such a remarkable woman. I can hear the guards returning; I must go to them at once. Good evening, Your Majesties, Your Highness. Thank you again for attending my ball." He bows, then walks outside in the direction of the stables.

Charming had spoken and left so quickly I didn't have time to fully process what he was saying. Mother's eyes flick between Father and King Kryler. "I'm sorry, but there must be a mistake. Prince Charming was meant to announce his engagement to my daughter tonight. This was established when Gertrude was born and has been honoured for the last eighteen years. We confirmed with you at dinner only last week.

Please explain why he is not going to maintain this arrangement?"

"I am sorry. I know as much as you do at this stage, Queen Cynthia. Please allow me the night to speak with my son and get to the bottom of this. I will attend you tomorrow, and we can discuss this at length," abruptly following after his son.

I had gone numb. This evening has gone pear shaped so quickly. I left their Castle in a daze, not paying any attention to my family or the journey home. I could see Mother and Father's mouths move as they spoke, but I couldn't hear what they said.

In my chambers, I quickly undressed, washed myself and fell into bed. I was lost within my thoughts, stumbling within the woods of my mind trying to find the exit, I fell into a fitful sleep, replaying the night's events over and over again. With one question floating in my mind.

Why?

* * *

*I*n my room, I saw King Kryler arrive and ushered into Fathers study five minutes ago. Not called or told of his visit, effectively excluding me from the discussion, I made a show of dressing to go to the gardens for a walk. *Why would I need to be involved? It's only my whole future they are discussing! Doesn't concern me at all!* Instead of heading out to the gardens, I loitered near Father's study and hid in an alcove away from prying eyes and listened to their conversation.

"I am sorry Mason, Charming is determined to find this 'Mystery Princess', as he is calling her. We have had this arrangement for eighteen years, and decades of friendship before that. Can you be lenient enough to allow me time to discuss it with him? I tried last night, but with the hour that the ball ended to now there hasn't been much time. I know you can understand how headstrong and stubborn he can be. He is a young Prince pushing his limits and trying to find himself. We have all been there. If you can grant me the time until he finds this woman and see what is to come of the situation? I believe once he finds her and the mystery is solved, he will give up his idea to marry the woman. In the meantime, I will be able to discuss his responsibilities further with him and remind him of his duty to marry Princess Gertrude." King Kryler pleaded.

"What does he hope to achieve? How can this woman be more beneficial for him than your allegiance with the Kingdom of Daes? Of course, we cannot hold off. We have promised you my daughter's hand since she was born. How are we to explain this to anyone? She will not be able to find a suitor now, for everyone will know she was dismissed by Charming. You must force Charming to keep his agreement. At least I can say my daughter knows her duty and will always put that first, unlike some people." I smiled softly. It was amusing hearing Father talk poorly about Charming and snubbing him on my behalf. Father had never stood up for me before, and it settled something in my heart to hear him defend me.

"Charming knows his duty," King Kryler interrupts, leaping to his son's defence. "Nevertheless, Gertrude is a beautiful woman and no one outside of our courts knew about their arrangement. She will still make someone a suitable wife."

"People expected it! With how close our Kingdoms are it has been the most predicted match of the last decade. Preparations have already been made for their wedding next week. He will ruin her if he does not give up this farse." Mother complains in a high pitch whine.

Father continues as if King Kryler and Mother hadn't spoken, "I will be tolerant and grant you time to go to him now. We will need to announce their engagement in the next few days to control the damage your son created and keep to their original wedding date. Everything is already organised and in place. To break this arrangement is going to sever all our agreements. I hope you understand that Kryler. Discuss this with Charming, are you sure he wants to commit an act of war over a mystery

'Princess'? You are his King and Father; can you not command him to keep his agreements?"

"You cannot be serious, Mason. Our Kingdoms have had alliances dating back hundreds of years. Don't be absurd, this does not need to destroy everything!"

"Your son is the future of your Kingdom. He is the one who will need to make and keep his agreements. If he is fickle with his commitments, if he cannot maintain an agreement as small and longstanding as a marriage, how can we trust him? How can we trust your Kingdom?"

"I'll handle it." King Kryler replied briskly storming out of the room.

Choosing to avoid my parent's wrath for now, I ease out of my hiding place and decide to continue my walk into the garden. I knew they weren't angry with me in this instance, yet previous experiences taught me, I would be their target to sling verbal abuse at until they felt better or had resolved the situation.

I aimlessly wandered around the gardens, passing the hours daydreaming about how the ball might have gone if the Mystery Princess hadn't had arrived. *How would be people take our announcement? Would we have enjoyed each other's company?* Would the image of him being so happy, yet losing that smile when he looked at me, ever leave my mind? When my feet grew tired, and my legs ached, I turned and headed towards my rooms. Deciding I needed dinner and an early night, I called my maid when I returned to my rooms and issued my orders.

Evalyn cleared her throat as she entered the room. Alerted to my return by the lady's maids no doubt.

"Where have you been? We have been looking for you for hours!" She scolds me like I am a petulant child, not an adult. I am so drained after all the events in the last twenty-four hours, I have no energy to pretend today. I didn't care what she thought of me.

"Obviously, not very hard," heavy sarcasm rolling off me.

"News arrived. Prince Charming found her, that 'Mystery

Princess' from last night. She is not a Princess at all! She was a lady who has been reduced to a servant to her step family, upon her father's death when she was a child." Evalyn continues ignoring my outburst. Relief coursed through me; she is a commoner. Surely, he will choose me over her. "Her name is Cinderella, and she is already married to Prince Charming."

"She's what?" I whisper in shock, frozen and barely able to find my voice.

"He married her! He found her this morning when King Kryler was here talking to King Mason and Queen Cynthia. He didn't tell King Kryler that he had found her, until he had already married her. King Kryler sent a letter two hours ago to King Mason, apologising for the broken engagement claiming there was nothing that he could do. He has offered for Prince Ambrose to wed you in Charming's stead, in an attempt to maintain the alliance and friendship between the Kingdoms." Rolling her eyes at the idea.

I am speechless. I was hurt last night when he ran off with her, but I genuinely thought all would be righted and he would end up with me. It is my duty and my salvation. Did he not think it was his duty to marry me for his Kingdom? And marrying Ambrose? I couldn't picture it. He was nicer than Charming, yet he had always seemed like a brother to me; I couldn't see us in bed together, living together. I would no longer be future Queen. I didn't need to be a Queen to be happy, I just needed to be away from this Palace. Being raised to be a Queen was all I knew though. It was my life's purpose and now I had nothing, no direction. At least marrying Ambrose would still get me away from Evalyn and Mother.

"What has Mother and Father said about Ambrose?"

"Your Father rejected the offer immediately. He no longer wants a connection with their Kingdom." She replies dismissively. "You should have been more engaging, more seductive. You lost to a common whore. Disgusting."

She storms from the room leaving me reeling. I no longer had a purpose or escape; I am stuck here.

I spend the night alone in my room, processing everything that has happened in the last twenty-four hours. Everything that I had been raised for was gone. I am not going to marry Charming. I am not going to be a Queen. I am not going to be leaving this Castle in a week's time. *I am not going to leave.* Will I ever be free?

Chapter Five

PRINCESS GERTRUDE

*M*other, Father and Harrison stare at me as I enter the study.

"Thank you for *finally* joining us Gertrude. I have called this meeting this morning to discuss the situation at hand. It is appalling that we have lost the allegiance with King Kryler, of their own faults and irresponsibility."

Chucking, Harrison interrupts, "to think, sister, Charming chose a peasant over you."

"Enough, Harrison," Father commanded, cutting off Harrison's laughter, "You are not at fault either!"

I sat silently showing no reaction to Harrison's dig, waiting for Father to continue and get to the point of our meeting.

"We need to start thinking about how we can salvage this situation. We now have an unattached eighteen-year old Princess, and a single Crown Prince. No one knew officially about the engagement with Charming. We need to get ahead of this before rumours get out of control. Cynthia, use the plans and decorations that were in place for the wedding next week, and invite all the Lords and Ladies we have connections with, and their eligible sons and daughters. We need to make a profitable arrangement."

"You brought this on yourself," Mother spoke directly to me. "If you weren't so sullen and closed off, you could have had him. He could have thought himself in love with you, not marrying the closest peasant to ensure he would be stuck with you." Mother's words cut though me like a knife, slicing me open right there on the study floor.

Turning back to Father, Mother continued discussing dinner party arrangements, balls and other events they could cart me off to. Where they could introduce me to eligible suitors and started making arrangements for who could replace Charming in taking me off their hands, as soon as possible.

With the meeting over, I found myself returning to the gardens. Charming and Cinderella are the lucky ones. Mother had said that he only married her to stop him from marrying me, but that couldn't be true. There were easier ways to break off a betrothal, or still marry me and have a mistress. He must actually love her. If they are happy, then maybe I will have my own shot at happiness and true love now too.

Enough is enough! No one should be responsible for my happiness, other than me. I will no longer play the meek Princess, content to listen and nod along with no opinions or voice. I was raised to be a Queen, damn it, and I am adamant to do what I need. To take my future into my own hands, and if I wasn't going to leave this Kingdom anytime soon, I need to see it. To know the lands, the villages and towns, the stories. To better know my people, be among them, and not above them.

Chapter Six

PRINCESS GERTRUDE

*T*hree Months Later
      Today is the first day of spring. I have always loved spring, all the blooming flowers and garden walks; it is truly the best time of the year. The last three months had been very trying for me. I was barely allowed outside of the Castle walls unless I was accompanied. Since Prince Charming married Cinderella, I have had to attend nonstop parties, events and meetings that Mother and Father hosted in the hopes of marrying me off as soon as possible. They had grown very jaded and hostile, making snide comments and slandering King Kryler and Prince Charming to anyone who would listen. After the initial shock had worn off, I could not find it in me to be upset that he called off the engagement. I had forgiven him almost as soon as I had learnt of their marriage. To have that kind of love and passion is my hearts only desire.

As I was not next in line to our throne, I am a tool that can be used to build connections and establish relationships with another Kingdom or powerful family. My duty is to serve my King in whatever he needs of me, that meant marrying anyone who benefited him the most.

I'm not sure what Mother and Father think of my lack of

proposals. Over the winter they introduced me to ten different suitors, and not one of them has lasted longer than a weekend. Maybe they think that as I was left by Prince Charming that I am not as wanted by other men? Little do they know that I have been sabotaging their attempts.

Due to the cold and snowy weather, winter had been the perfect time for them to host small gatherings or weekend visitors. Each weekend had followed the same path. On Friday night, a Lord or Prince, or some other high-ranking nobleman that my Father approved of, attended our Castle for dinner. Often a suitor for Harrison would also join us, allowing Mother and Father to play matchmaker for both of us. They were provided with enough personal time to form an attachment to us. Then were invited to stay in the Castle for the weekend, to which was readily agreed to and they happened to oh so conveniently have brought a trunk with them, with enough formal and social wear to last the weekend. Joining in with a full family breakfast, he would join with the men's activities, hunting or sport of some kind, and she would join myself and mother.

Afterwards they would swap, he would find me for my afternoon walk on Saturday. I am not sure what Harrison did to entertain his lady friends. On Saturday night, we had a formal dinner that included dancing with our family and court, then Harrison and I each had a private breakfast on Sunday with our prospective partners. No doubt by design of my Mother or Father, assuming that they would like to make their declarations of love in secret. Ending with a "we hope to see you again soon" farewell from the whole court.

The following days saw my Father receiving a letter from the suitor summarising a "thank you for having me", "Gertrude was great, but no I will not be pursuing her". In my family's presence, I was the perfect Princess, I went along with their plan for these random men to meet and marry me, showing no signs of objection or refusal to enter such an engagement.

However, while alone with the gentlemen on Sunday mornings, I spoke with each of them directly and plainly, then sent them on their way. By gentleman number three I basically had a script memorised that I recited.

"You have been summoned to this Castle, by my Father, to marry me. Have you not?" I ask directly, conveying no excitement or happy emotion at the idea of them wanting to marry me. Receiving a "Yes, Your Highness" in response, except for Lord Embry who said, "No actually, Your Highness, I reached out to him and asked if I would be graced with the honour of an invitation." Lord Embry was the most difficult one to get rid of, but I persisted and was victorious in the end

"You see, Sir, you do not want to marry me. My Father and Brother have plans to marry me off for the most valuable trade. You will be tied to this family and Kingdom, but you or your children will never sit on the throne or reap the benefits of your allegiance with Daes. I may be beautiful, but that will fade. I am highly intelligent, but not at general life. I was raised to be Queen and have standards and expectations that need to be met. I am not a quiet or easy soul; I will cause havoc in your household. I will not be put on another leash, and paraded around for you, to be glad that you captured the Princess' heart. I can assure you that we will not be happy together. I will not come willingly to your bed. I will not make this arrangement go easily for you. I will not abide by any restrictions you place on me, my life or my body. I will not submit to you, not only because I out rank you, but because I have a mind and a soul that demands more. I will not settle for less than I deserve. I suggest that you go and find yourself the docile and submissive wife that you are looking for. I also suggest that it is in your best interest to not inform my family of this discussion, as not only will I deny it happened, but no one will believe you. As you should have noticed by now, I am an amazing actress and have my whole family convinced that I have no mind of my own, and they will not think me capable of having this conversation with you."

They all left after that speech; the only protest came from

Lord Embry. Reiterating how I would never be under his thumb and how he would never have my family wrapped around his finger, he eventually gave up too. With the end of winter, more suitors would come, from further distances that could now travel again.

I am getting over the constant barrage of men everywhere and decided today was a perfect day to go on an adventure and live up to the promise I made myself to explore my own Kingdom.

During my youth, I had many day trips out into Prince Charming's Kingdom. Mother was always encouraging me to get to know the lands and the subjects who I would one day rule. Escorted by Evalyn, I went on several shopping adventures, and site seeing all over the Kingdom. I visited all the galleries, museums, plays and shows exhibiting arts that I could manage. The only downside to all this, I never got to see my own Kingdom. I never really thought about it much until the Cinderella event. I am eighteen, no longer engaged to marry a Prince and become Queen, and I don't know my own Kingdom at all.

Over the winter I really had the time to analyse my life, now that so much had changed, and it was time for me to figure out what I wanted to do with it. I honestly still don't know what I want to do with my life, but I know I want to see my Kingdom.

I rose early today, determined to get out of the Castle before anyone else woke. Dressed in my navy riding habit, wearing a long skirt and cropped jacket that stopped at my waist, black boots and black gloves, I walk quietly down the hall and outside the Palace. Not having any maids to assist me dress this morning, I have left my hair in the simple braid that I slept in. I had chosen today's outfit very carefully, appearing as a wealthy and respectable Lady, but not the Princess. I was not in the mood for people to bow and scrape for me today, not that I was ever really in the mood for that. I want to be among the people and get to know them as one of them, not who they pretended to be when royalty was around. Wearing no jewellery or broaches that could tip anyone off to who my family was.

Making my way down to the stables where my mare Stormy was housed, I thought back to when I was gifted Stormy as a child. She was born of other horses in the palace stables and is now thirteen years old. Stormy is an Andalusian mare who is sixteen hands, and towers over me. She has a beautiful pale and dark grey coat which flows like storm clouds, with dark a long and wavy grey mane and tail, and deep brown eyes. I named her Stormy due to the combination of her colouring and her personality. She would change as quickly as a storm could roll in. One minute a calm and placid creature, the next a wild beast. I loved that the trainer couldn't break that part of her spirit. I was the only one she would calm down for. Stormy is my best, and probably only, friend.

"Hello," I call to the stable boy.

"Good Morning, Your Highness," he replies bowing.

"Should anyone from the household enquire where I am, will you please advise that I have gone for a ride?" I ask him, walking to Stormy. I was used to spending lots of time out with Stormy in the warmer months, and whenever my responsibilities and duties allowed it. It wasn't uncommon for me to take Stormy out for a long ride, and I was hoping that Mother and Father wouldn't ask where I was until later into the day. I had never left the palace grounds alone, always accompanied while on rides or travelling to events. Thankfully, the boy did not question me on that.

"Of course, Your Highness" the boy replied. He was familiar with me after all the time I spent here with Stormy. He left me in peace while I went about my routine of brushing her down, feeding her, giving Stormy a once over check and preparing her in her saddle for a day's ride.

After ensuring I had money, water and food for myself in my saddle bags, I set off on Stormy to go and explore my home, my country, my Kingdom.

Chapter Seven

PRINCESS GERTRUDE

*A*lthough, I have never been alone in the Kingdom, I knew my way around after years of studying maps and escorted trips. I set off east from the stables, heading through the Jang Forest in the direction of Mount Ters. It is said the village Adaira, at the bottom of the mountain, had beautiful creations by artists and woodworkers. Although I had stopped their several times before while travelling to Prince Charming's Kingdom, I had never travelled into the village. Art is something I have always taken pleasure in, enjoying finding the unique and beautiful expressions of each artist. I have a collection of little artworks in the Gallery at our Palace, and I have several from Prince Charming's Kingdom. Remembering with a pang that I have none from my own Kingdom. That was going to change, starting with today's adventure.

The journey to Adaira takes me four hours on Stormy; we stopped for a break halfway there to allow Stormy to have a drink and myself some breakfast. Adaira was only forty kilometres from the palace, and I knew Stormy could have gotten us there faster, but I am enjoying travelling at a leisurely walk. The Jang Forest is alive, and all the animals are animated with spring. Babies follow their mothers around, learning how to walk and forage. Reminding me this is the first time I have been completely alone in my life. No guards or maids loitering around. Rejoicing in my temporary freedom, I lie in a bed of wildflowers. Colours of blues, pinks, yellows and oranges are everywhere, and I collect a handful to take back to the palace with me.

Continuing our adventure, we arrive in Adaira around ten in the morning, timed perfectly with all the villagers it seemed. Everyone was out and about accomplishing several tasks for the day.

I dismount Stormy near the village stables, hoping that they will have space to house her during my stay in the village.

"Good Morning, Ma'am. Welcome to Adaira." A boy of about thirteen calls out while walking over to where I am standing with Stormy near the stable entrance. He is a bit taller than me and wide set with a toned muscular frame I can just make out though his shabby plaid shirt and overalls. His shaggy, ashy hair squished under a cap.

"Good Morning," I reply suppressing my sigh of pleasure. It is nice to not hear *Your Highness*. "I was wondering if this is where I would be able to hold my horse, Stormy, for a few hours while I explored the village?" I ask him, smiling and showing my joy.

"How long are you here to visit? You are welcome to store your horse here. Our costs are either per day or per hour depending on your needs."

"Only here for a few hours today, thank you."

After setting up my account with the stable boy, I removed my coin purse from Stormy's saddle bag, and let her be taken into a stable for the next few hours.

I planned on trotting Stormy back to the palace, making our journey home faster. To ensure I was home by tea, I only had three hours in the village before I needed to leave. The village is set up in a neat and orderly lay out, with the stables being near the west entrance. Walking down the main street, there are several houses with small yards, each house unique in design and structure. Some houses are flat and long, while others are tall and wide. Several houses are made of wood logs, where others are from brick or stone of various colours. Each house did have one thing in common, they all showed signs of being loving and happy homes. Children are running around, playing and helping maintain household chores, mothers or fathers watching over them, teaching them life lessons and the ways of the world. I can feel eyes watching me as I make my way through the town, and I knew that the whole village would know I was here within five minutes.

The village is not as large as I expected, after a few hundred metres, by the centre water well I found the town hall, the church and the art gallery buildings. There are three art gallery buildings that are connected with long thin hallways. From what I read; each showcased a different type of artwork. The one on the right should house all the paintings and drawings. The building on the left holds all clay and marble sculptures, and the one in the middle housed all wood carvings and leather works.

Walking into the centre gallery building, I find a young woman sitting behind the front desk. She is dressed in an elegant and flowing soft yellow dress, her blonde hair curled into a tight bun, held at the base of her skull. She is all smiles, her eyes twinkling in the morning sunlight that came through the open door.

"Good Morning, Miss. If I may introduce myself, my name is Rosemary Smithers. I am the daughter of the village President, Earnest Smithers, and I look after the galleries here. Can I help you with anything today?" She had a soft sweet voice that makes me feel warm like standing in the sunshine.

"Good day Rosemary, my name is Trudy..." I paused, what last name should I give? I hadn't thought of that. I could not provide her with Daes; it would surely click within seconds that I am related to the Royal Family of Daes. *What can my name be!?* Ambrose popped into my head. "Uh, Kn-kni-knight. Trudy Knight." I said while stuttering slightly. "It's lovely to meet you. I travelled here today as I heard you had a vast collection of art that I would like to see, and even look into acquiring."

"Oh really?" Rosemary replied, shock and sadness colouring her voice. "We currently do not have any works for sale. My father can provide you with the artists contact information for commissions or work they may have for sale personally. Prince Charming travelled through here on his honeymoon with Princess Cinderella and she loved them. He bought every piece we had and is allowing us to keep displaying them until he returns to the Castle to organise delivery."

Jealousy and confusion race through me. Why did he come to Adaira? It is near the border of his Kingdom. Yet, to come here after calling off his engagement with me, with the situation between our Fathers'? I thought he would be more cautious.

"Why would he do that? Their Kingdom is full of artists, why would he need to buy these pieces?" Charming had never bought me anything, or cared about what interested me, though our betrothal. One more sign that we never loved each other.

"It is not for us to assume, Miss Knight. I am sure he had his reasons, as all Royals do for everything they do," She grew defensive. "They are all lovely pieces, maybe they do not have work as great as these in their Kingdom."

"I do not mean to offend you, Rosemary. I am upset they stole the chance for me to purchase today. Do the King and Queen of Daes know of his visit?" I ask, trying to not give away how interested I am. How will Father take his visit to our Kingdom?

"I do not know, Miss. My Father sent them a letter after it happened two weeks ago, to my knowledge we are yet to receive a response or action from Their Majesties. They have always been close with Prince Charming's family; I presume they know about it and do not care about what it means to an outreach village of little to no consequence in their Kingdom." Rosemary's face blooming into a bright red, she slams her mouth shut, clearly remembering that she is speaking with a stranger and that these comments are treasonous. "I apologise, Miss Knight, I do not mean to say such things. Please, disregard that. I do not mean to speak ill of the royal families."

"Please Rosemary, call me Trudy. I'm sorry, I simply cannot forget what you have said," her face crumples in displeasure, and I can feel a smile tugging at my lips as I continue "it is the most honest and truthful thing anyone has ever said to me. I agree wholeheartedly. I think you just became my favourite person," excitement lacing my voice, Rosemary gave me an enquiring look. I have a feeling we will be fast and close friends.

"You agree with me?" she asks tentatively.

"Yes, I do. Now are you able to give me a tour?"

"Of course!" she responds with glee and a mischievous smile. Oh! Yes, I think we will be great friends. "I know everything about every work in these galleries."

Linking arms with Rosemary, we walk into the gallery. She shows me the clay and marble sculptures first, before moving on to the drawings and paintings, and finishing with the carvings and leather works. One of the wood carvings caught my attention, and I was fixed upon it. It was a horse about the size of my torso. The face, mane and hair of the horse were so detailed and realistic.

"That is made by a relatively local artist. He has provided us with many art pieces over the years. This is a carving of this father's horse, made when the artist was seventeen years old."

I am amazed at the skill, detail and care the artist has put into this work. Clearly Rosemary was able to tell how in love I am with this work.

"Unfortunately, he doesn't take commissions."

Crestfallen, I continue looking around the galleries, still in shock that Prince Charming bought all these works. Where did he plan on putting them in his Castle? His gallery was already full. I had seen the space many times in my visits to his Castle.

"Rosemary, when will your father be available for me to discuss this artist's information with him? Am I able to go on a wait list if this artist ever comes to you with work again?" I ask unable to contain my excitement at the prospect of owning his work.

"I do not know, Trudy. He is out of the village today handling a problem. Would you be able to stay here for the night? I am sure you would be able to speak with him tomorrow."

"Unfortunately, not, Rosemary, I have prior arrangements and must be home tonight. Would you be able to talk with him about me, and let him know I will be back in three days' time? I would appreciate it if he would be here for me to meet then. Do you think that would be possible and enough notice for him to clear time for me?"

"I will talk to him tonight, Trudy, and ensure he is here for your return."

"I feel a fast friendship forming with us Rosemary. I have not had a real friend before, and I look forward to seeing you again soon."

If Rosemary was shocked by my bluntness, she didn't show it.

"Yes, Trudy. I look forward to your return as well." We part ways outside of the gallery, Rosemary has to stay to look after them as myself back through the village to the stables.

I feel so free, today I have been Trudy, and I was liked. I had made a friend. My smile could not be shaken from my face.

Chapter Eight

PRINCESS GERTRUDE

J spend the journey home thinking about what it would be like to be so loved by Charming that he bought all those art pieces for me, and what works I could commission to have made by the artists. Cinderella was lucky to have found someone so thoughtful after all she had been through. In the month after their wedding a lot of rumours had joined us at the gatherings Mother and Father hosted. Stories telling of how her mother passed, having her father remarry, and her father passing leaving her alone with her step mother and two step sisters. She was treated awfully by them, locked in rooms, forced to do all the chores in her own house after her step mother fired all the servants, forbidding her to be a part of their family and be seen in public with them. For her to have overcome that all and found it in her to love and trust. She must be very brave. I wish I could be brave like her.

I am especially interested in seeing if Mr Smithers could persuade the wood carver to sell to me. My stomach is full of anxious butterflies. Do I buy this work as Trudy Knight or Princess Gertrude? Do I let the villagers know who I am? Rosemary seemed like a lovely person, and I am glad to have met her. Hope fills me at the idea of me having my first true friend, one who was not influenced by my title, or are in my parent's pocket just hoping to get something out of me.

Suddenly, I notice there is no noise at all coming from the forest. Looking around, there are no animals, no wind, rustle of leaves or branches. I tilt my head to the sky, to see if there is an incoming storm, but cannot make it out through the tree tops. Panic ceases me, the trees and road are not familiar. I cannot remember if this is the way that we came into Adaira. Thinking back, I definitely took the right road when I left the village. I must have taken a wrong turn when I was lost inside my thoughts. It's not the first time it has happened, I get lost within myself all the time while walking around the gardens at the Palace. This are different than my gardens though, there are no sign posts or clear paths to walk on. The forest has more trees and shrubbery than I had seen on my way to Adaira, I have never seen this part of the Jang Forest before. The continued silence is unsettling, I need to get out of this area now.

"Come on Stormy. Let's turn back and see if I can find the right way this time." Glad I could at least hear myself speak, I turn Stormy around, and hear a soft clang. If the forest were not so quiet, I probably would not have heard it. "What was that?" I ask Stormy dismounting to find the source of the sound. Looking around the forest floor, I found it. A horse shoe.

"Oh no!" I groan aloud, reaching down to check Stormy's hooves, finding that she has thrown a shoe! Just my luck today. Who knew how far behind me Adaira is? The Palace will be hours away riding, let alone walking. If I can figure out where I am, perhaps I can get back to Adaira. Adaira has a blacksmith next to the stables, they will be able to fix her a new shoe. "Come on, then." I say to Stormy, beginning our walk back to Adaira.

* * *

*W*ith no markers or signs around, I am utterly lost in the woods. I don't know which direction I need to head in to get back to Adaira. Looking around the tree-tops for a gap or clearing that I could head too, I saw a large streak of sunlight off to my right. "What harm can it do, hey Stormy?" I said while leading Stormy towards the break in the trees. I had learnt how to guide myself by the sun and to know the time and direction in which I was facing from my riding instructor, Matthew, when I was eleven years old. Over and over again he would say, *"Knowing your way is the most important thing to remember, Your Highness. You mastered riding Stormy and the other horses; you need to ensure that you can always find your way."*

"Much good it does me now, Matthew," I mutter to the empty forest.

Coming closer, I realise the gap was much bigger than I expected. Breaking through the trees I stand at the edge of a large rectangular field filled with dead grass, leading on for around a hundred meters and with two buildings at the far end. The sun is low in the sky and indicating it is roughly three in the afternoon. Much later than I had hoped, I needed to be back at the palace by five for tea.

Leading Stormy, I walk towards the buildings while my eyes scan the field. Hopefully, someone lived here and could help us. Getting closer to the buildings I can make out one is cabin and the other is a barn. I lead Stormy up to the cabin and leaving her free on the grass to rest, I step up on the wraparound porch. My boots click loudly against the wooden steps, echoing as I walk to the front door. I raise my hand to knock and hesitate, taking a deep breath to settle my nerves, it could be empty, or a horrible person could live here. I am a Princess; I have no need for nerves. I will simply knock on the door and ask for help. *Be brave.*

"WHAT THE *FUCK* DO YOU WANT?!" a deep male voice yells from within the cabin.

"Well, there's definitely someone living here," I mutter to myself. He sounds enraged. Ducking my head, I chew on my bottom lip, perhaps this is a bad idea. I should leave now before he comes outside. Heavy steps clomp through the cabin, getting louder as the owner makes his way to the door. Before I can retreat, the door flies open, almost ripped off its hinges.

With my head still down, two large black boots step into my eye sight as he leans though the door frame. *Too late to leave now!* Squaring my shoulders, I lift my head allowing my eyes to take in the length of his body. He is wearing faded black trousers that has tears over his thighs and knees, and a red plaid long sleeve shirt that is unbuttoned to show a bare chest with fair chest hair, six-pack abs and a whole lot of muscle. Taking in his body, my breathing quickens, I cannot find my voice. He is about five foot eight to my five feet, his skin tanned from days in the sun. He has long dirty blonde hair held back with a piece of leather, and odd strands falling loose around his face. His face captivated me. What I am assuming is a strong chiselled jaw is covered in a beard the same shade as his hair, his strong eyebrows casting shadows over bright sea green eyes. My breath catches in my throat as we make eye contact.

"Who the fuck are you?" he asks in a gruff voice.

You wanted an adventure.

Chapter Nine

PRINCESS GERTRUDE

I stand there for a moment, attempting to compose myself and figuring out how to respond to that question. Who do I want to be to this man? Princess or commoner?

"Well I don't have all day, woman!" his deep rumbling voice drawing me out of my thoughts. *Be brave.*

"I'm sorry to bother you, Sir...? My horse threw a shoe, and I am lost, how can I get to Adaira from here?" No matter how attractive he was, I need to keep away from him. I have trained for political battles and have been handling men with their needs and wishes for months now. Just because this man was a bit more realistic, and rougher than the men attending me in the palace shouldn't change the way he affects me.

"I don't give a shit. That's not my problem. Leave. Now." he barks in order while starting to close the cabin door. Clearly, I was correct in my judgement to not let his attractiveness sway me, he is an asshole.

"Now wait a moment." I slam my hand into the door, preventing him from closing it in my face, a sharp pain throbbing under my glove against the wood. Not letting the pain show, I put my bitchy alter ego on full display, "Would it be that hard to just point me in the right direction, so I can get off your porch and away from you? Or would you rather I sit here, encroaching on your space until someone comes to find me, and can assist me in getting home?"

He looks incredulous. Well, he can go to hell. He deserves to be treated this way, if this is how he treats helpless strangers on his property. He assesses me, as if he were trying to figure out where I found the audacity to speak to him like that.

"I don't like having to repeat myself. Who the fuck are you?" His deep smooth voice washes over me again. I am going to get lost inside that voice if I can't control myself.

"Well, who the fuck are you?" I respond haughtily. I have never said fuck out loud. Ever. Not even alone in the Palace, with all of those listening ears. I knew the word, but I had never said it.

His eyes widen in what I assume is shock that a woman of my appearance would know such words; let alone have the capacity to speak them aloud, or the recklessness to speak to him in such a way. His eyes appraise me, taking in my body in an obvious glance and lingering on my breasts and waist. My core clenches knowing his eyes are on me. I have never had a reaction like this to a man; he is going to be dangerous to be around.

"Ika." The name rolls off his tongue, as a smooth whiskey. Of course, the sexy man had a sexy as hell name to go with the rest of him. Was I due for bad karma? Meeting him today, in a bad mood and having no hope to... what? Seduce him? Scoffing at the thought, why would I want that? Other than the fact he was attractive. Unless he was like this every day, I am not sure if the idea of finding that out is exciting to me or not. My mind is telling me I should leave Ika in peace and never see him again, but there is a feeling I can't place when I look at him.

"Trudy," If he is not going to provide a last name, then neither will I. Petty and childish, maybe, but as an eighteen-year old who never had much of a childhood, could anyone really blame me? I stare him down, maintaining eye contact, not letting his intensity waver me. What is this man's problem? "So, Adaira...? Can you tell me how to get there?"

Ika looked like he was hurt and confused by me.

"I do not go there anymore, and I will not show you the way. There is nothing worthwhile there now."

Trying to not let my desperation show, "You don't need to show me the way, just point me in the right direction and I can find my own way."

An amused smirk spreads across Ika's face breaking through the scowl he has had since he opened the door, "Like you found your way here?"

I could feel my cheeks heating in embarrassment, "Excuse you, but I can direct myself; I just couldn't see the sun." I don't know why I am explaining myself to this man.

"Either way it doesn't matter, Darlin'." His drawl shortening his words.

"And why is that?"

"There ain't no one in Adaira who can help you."

"Yes, yes there is. I have been to Adaira."

"I think you are mistaken, girl."

I chuckle, the stress starting to get to me, "Surely, you can't be serious? Do you get off on causing distress in others? Please just tell me where to go, or I will leave and find someone else who will be able to help me. I need to get back to the main market next to the Palace of Daes. "

I turn and walk off the porch, as he stands there watching me. I have a feeling he is gauging the situation, at war with himself thinking about what he should do. As if some alpha male part of him wants to ensure I get home safely, and the asshole part wants me to leave him alone.

Groaning, he spoke as I reached Stormy, "Wait. I'll show you the way. We'll have to walk. I have no horse or ability to fix her shoe. Sit there," he indicated a rocking chair on the porch, "wait there until I return. I'll gather some supplies." He grumbled shutting the door as he went back into the cabin. Walking back onto the porch I sat down in the rocking chair and looked out over the field and the forest beyond and could even see Mount Ters in the distance. This place is so peaceful. I could imagine this being a favourite spot to sit and read or watch the sunset.

Ika returns walking around from the back of the cabin, holding a large black bag. Stepping up beside Stormy, he introduces himself before hoisting up the bag to rest on Stormy's back and securing it to her saddle. Holding her reins in one hand, he looks at me over his shoulder, "Come on then, Darlin'. We need to move if we are going to get anywhere before nightfall."

Chapter Ten

PRINCESS GERTRUDE

We set off in a brisk walk, the pace not allowing for much in the way of conversation. Trying to recover from the whiplash his reactions had given me I paid more attention to the path, memorising our surroundings.

"Why did you change your mind and decide to take me to Adaira?" I'm sure he is crazy, and yet I feel safe enough to let him lead me back into the woods?

"I'm not taking you to Adaira. I already told you I don't go there."

Stopping in my tracks I call after him, "Then where are we going?"

"To where you want to go. The main market." Ika keeps walking, not waiting for me to catch up. We fall silent, taking turns to lead Stormy.

"We are about to lose daylight. We need to make camp for the night, and we can continue the journey in the morning." Ika spoke, shocking me suddenly hearing his deep voice again after so long.

"Spend the night? In the forest?" The idea of spending the night with Ika unsettles me. I have never spent a night away from the Palace. Who knows what he could do to me while I sleep?

"Not like we have many options, Darlin'."

I hadn't told anyone where I was going this morning when I left the palace, would anyone be looking for me yet? Had they even noticed I was gone?

I'm sure Mother and Father would understand when I explained it if I ever get home. It's not like I could have done anything differently, I checked her shoes before I left the palace this morning. I debate asking Ika to continue on tonight, though I'm too exhausted after just an eventful day.

Ika led Stormy to a tree at the edge of a small clearing, removing her saddle and his bag.

"There is a stream down to the right, feel free to clean up or get a drink while I set up the camp."

Unloading some lumpy fabric rolls that I could not identify, food and some weapons from his bag.

"They are only for catching dinner." Answering my silent question in a flat voice, not looking up from his supplies. How did he even know I was watching him? Leaving him to it, I need a moment alone to digest all that has happened today, I collect my empty water skin and Stormy and walk down to the stream Ika mentioned.

The stream is broken by a wide and deep rock pool, which has clean clear water. So clear that you can see all the fish swimming around at the bottom of the pool. The water runs over the rocks making a small waterfall into the pool. Removing my gloves and rolling up my jacket sleeves, I quickly refill my water skin, leaving Stormy to drink.

Heading back to the camp, I begin collecting chunks of wood and fallen branches. We will need a fire tonight, and gathering firewood is a task I have never done before. This would be a mundane everyday chore for someone like Ika, and I find myself wanting to help as much as possible, to show him that we are be equals. I don't know why it was suddenly important to me to prove it to him. He doesn't know I am a Princess. He didn't need to swoop in and save me as some damsel, yet he was helping me. Gathering firewood is a small step in returning the favour, but it is a start.

Re-entering the clearing with Stormy, Ika looks up and meets my gaze, "Good, you're back. You didn't get lost this time," a smirk breaking across his face.

Scowling at him, I drop all the firewood next to where he is standing, then tie Stormy up to the same tree as Ika had earlier, giving her enough space to sit down or graze should she wish. "I just had to follow the distinct smell of bastard to find my way back to you, Ika." I say in a sweet voice that doesn't match my expression. *Why are you antagonising him? He is your only chance of getting to the Palace.*

He ignores me, thankfully, and points at the firewood. "Thanks for that. You can get started on the fire while I go find some food then." He stalks towards the stream so quickly I don't have the chance to respond. I haven't any idea how to start a fire. I had never had to before. Huffing in anger, I follow after him. Couldn't he tell that I wasn't the type of woman who knew how to start fires?

I stomp back to the rock pool, making no effort to conceal the noise of my steps through the fallen leaves and branches on the forest floor. I reach the break through the last of the trees, and see his boots are unlaced and placed haphazardly at the foot of a tree. Passing the tree, I step out onto the rocky creek bank and freeze in my tracks. Out in the creek is Ika standing up to his knees in water, naked. The defined muscles of his arms tense as he pulls his long fingers through his unbound dripping wet hair, falling to his waist. My eyes follow the length of his hair down to his tight, shapely, perfect ass. Supported by long powerful legs. I see his muscles tense as he shifts, drawing my gaze to the drops of water running down his body from his hair.

His chuckle breaks my trance, and I quickly flick my eyes

back up and meet his gaze over his shoulder. He had seen me staring at him, in all his naked glory.

"Enjoying the show there, Trudy? Should I turn around for you to get the full view? Or were you out here to join me instead?" He asks, his voice huskier than usual, his expression conveying he was serious and would turn if I asked him too.

Yes! "No!" I scream out, "I came to tell you that I cannot light a fire, so you will need to do it."

"Of course, milady," he replies, amusement colouring his voice, all traces of huskiness gone. "Anything else that you would like to command me to do while you are at it?"

"Other than requesting you put your clothes back on before returning to camp, no." Turning on my heel, I walk back to the camp. I don't understand why I let him rule me. He is a strange backwoods man. I have tackled Palace discussions and raised to be Queen. I should be able to handle a simple man. A man who makes my core melt, who has the body of a god, and who makes my knees weak with a single glance. He is so strange, unique and unlike anyone I know. I want to hit him and sit on his face in the same breath. He has my mind and my stomach doing back flips. Entering the camp, I pat Stormy, using her as a barrier between Ika. I need to control myself before I do something stupid, like throw myself at him.

Chapter Eleven

PRINCESS GERTRUDE

*I*ka returned to the camp about twenty minutes later. His long hair is still wet but is now braided down his spine and dressed. Like at his cabin, his six-pack and muscular torso are bare to me through his open shirt. My eyes stick to him, studying like I want to memorize this view. Distracted by his body, it takes me a moment to realise that he did not return empty-handed. Ika has three grey scaled fish hanging from his left hand.

Does he not like to be clothed properly? Ika places the fish on a piece of cloth next to his supplies off to the left of the clearing.

"No, he does not." Ika chuckles with a grin, breaking through my revelry.

"I said that out loud?" I ask, my embarrassment showcased by my blush.

"You sure did, Darlin'. Do you do that often? Speak to yourself mentally, and have said it out loud?"

"I'm not really sure. I don't spend a lot of time around other people for them to either respond or point it out to me." Adverting my gaze, I feel stupid. Ika doesn't know me. His opinion should mean nothing to me, and yet I don't want him to see what everyone else sees. The heartless Princess.

Picking up on my tone and body language, Ika thankfully lets the topic drop

"So, do you want to learn how to light a fire or not?" Ika asks, starting towards the firewood I had collected earlier. Collecting a portion of the wood, he starts arranging it into a carefully organised pile in the middle of the clearing.

"You want to teach me how to light a fire?"

"Sure Darlin', it's a good skill to have." Elated, I nod at him and watch his hands work as he continues speaking, "First you have to prepare the woodpile, and load it with kindling. The kindling is what the fire is going to grab onto the easiest. We need to ensure that there is enough that the wood will have enough time to start burning before the kindling runs out," talking through the motions, explaining what he is doing. "This is a flint and steel," showing me the tools that produces from his bag, "I want you to have a go at trying to light the fire."

"Uh, are you sure? I don't want to set the forest alight or anything. Are you sure you can trust me?" trying and failing to conceal my anxiety.

"How are you going to learn something, if you never do it, Darlin'?" He asks, his deep rumbling voice warming me up inside. Walking over, I watch his hands, as he shows me how to use the tools. Handing me the flint and steel, I follow his steps and attempt to light the fire. I am a perfectionist, it came with the territory of being a Princess, I suppose. Frustrated, I struggled, using the striking stone as Ika had instructed, with no spark. Suddenly, Ika wraps his body around mine, his hands holding mine around the tools. I loosen my grip on the tools, assuming he was going to take over.

Instead, surprising me, he tightens my hands around the tools. "Hold them like this, Darlin'." He whispered into my ear. "Just relax, move your wrist like this," he instructs while moving my hands and arms as he needs. Finally, the flint and steel hit the right way and creates a spark settling the kindling alight.

"Oh, my gosh," I breathe out. "I did it!" I squeak unflatteringly. I turn inside his arms that are still wrapped around me and hug him. "Thank you! Thank you for letting me try, for teaching me."

"Yeah you did, Darlin', and s'ok." He pulls back and I can see shock written all over his face. Dropping his arms, he turns and heads towards the fish.

"The fire needs time to take and heat up, while we wait for that I am going to prepare the fish so we can cook that for dinner." Ika explains, relishing how he doesn't condescend me but explains what he is doing in a helpful and instructive manner. Returning to the fire, Ika goes about setting some sticks into the ground that he explains he will use to cook. We don't talk as he prepares the fish; I close my eyes and take a deep breath, falling to a short meditation and enjoying the sounds of the forest around us and the crackling fire.

"I am sure that this is nothing like the fine foods you're probably used to, Trudy. Plain fish cooked over a campfire cannot really compare to much of the rich folks' food. It will be enough to rid you of your hunger tonight, and we will have you dining back in splendour soon enough. Think of this as an adventure. How can you really know the quality of fine foods, if you haven't tasted what the commoners eat, aye?" He talks plainly without a hint of contempt or anger at the fact that I wouldn't have eaten like this before. It's like he can read my mind and know what I had left my Palace for.

"Yes," I reply wryly, meeting his gaze, "an adventure indeed."

"How about a campfire story as we cook and eat?" I am assuming he wants to torture me some more by telling me a scary story. Or hoping I will chicken out before he even started.

"Go ahead," I challenge.

"Have you heard the story of the Mystery Princess?" he asks me, while rotating the fish over the fire.

"No. I have not." I reply uncertainly.

Offering me a small smile he begins the story, "Four autumns past, Prince Charming was celebrating his twenty-first birthday in royal fashion with an extravagant ball. For decades, the Kingdom of Daes have been close with his Father, and everyone was expecting an announcement to be made at the ball, of Prince Charming's engagement to the Princess of Daes, Gertrude Daes." m

"What do you mean four autumns past?!" I exclaim, cutting him off abruptly. Did Ika suspect who I am and was trying to get me to admit it? That only happened a few months ago, not years. Is he trying to catch me in my lie about who I am?

Ika looks at me with a hard, inquisitive look. "What day is it, Trudy?"

"It's the first day of spring." I reply rolling my eyes.

"How old is Prince Charming?"

"Twenty-one, in the autumn just gone, not four years ago."

Ika's eyes go wide, "How long were you lost in the woods for, Trudy?"

"Uh, a couple of hours? I left Adaira at about one in the afternoon. I needed to ensure I had enough time to travel to get home for tea. You can see how well that plan worked out." I add while waving my hand at the camp around us.

"I have something to tell you. You will think I am crazy, and I don't blame you for it. You will realise I am telling the truth when we get back to your house." He pauses. "The Silent Wood is cursed."

I break out in laughter. "Sure, it is, and this is not just another campfire story to try and scare me." I interject sarcastically.

"Listen, woman! It *is* cursed. When you are trapped in the forest, time goes slower for you, but continues at a normal rate outside. It has never been confirmed what the exact difference is, but we find it works out to roughly one year for every half an hour in the forest. I would hazard a guess and say you entered that forest at least four years ago. Given that King Charming has been married for four years now and is now King when you think him a Prince, I think it is safe to assume I am right." He looks both smug at being right and conflicted at the information that I have essentially been trapped in a forest for four years.

"You're right." I admit. "You are completely insane. How can you say such fantastical things? Where do you create it? I don't imagine you as much of a storyteller."

"Fine, woman," Ika replies, not attempting to conceal his agitation and anger. "You do not need to believe me, when you return home you will see that I was right, and that everyone probably assumes you have been missing for four years, dead, or do you not have anyone to return home to? Do you not have anyone that would be concerned that you have been missing for four years?" He is trying to aggravate me, to trick me into telling him more about myself. His words strum a chord in me. If he is right, would my family be wondering about where I have been? Would they think I ran away or had died? Shaking myself from those thoughts I remind myself that Ika is crazy and I have only been gone a day. Even still, with being gone for a day would they have noticed?

"What about you then? You were alone in that cabin of yours. Don't you have anyone who cares about you? You didn't need to say goodbye to anyone before we left or make any arrangements to check on your household or any livestock. So, either you have no one, or hidden servants."

"I live alone. I prefer my solitude. I have been alone since my father died when I was eighteen, seven years ago. I do not require any servants. I don't have any animals at my cabin, as I don't need any. I don't run a farm or need to have any livestock; I don't grow produce or need anything for farming. Where is your home, by the way? You never said anything other than you were heading to the main market."

I look away from his face, and those prying bright eyes. What am I thinking? I know he will eventually find out who I am, but I don't want him to know yet. I have enjoyed being free of my title and the weight that comes with it. Putting it off as much as possible will bite me when he finds out, but I don't want to be there when he realises who I am. I don't want to see the reaction it brings. Will he be shocked? Will he turn into one of those fools who fall over themselves in my presence? I couldn't tell why it is important for me that he knows who the real Trudy is. It has been in the back of my mind since we met, and I am determined for him to not know who I am until he knows the woman behind the title.

"You will find out when we get there." I respond in a vain attempt to delay the inevitable "That is, if it is still there. If what you have to say is true and I have been missing for four years, maybe my home will not be there anymore. It could have new occupants, or my family may not want me back and will cast me away to never return as they have been happy the last four years without me."

He looks at me, those vibrant green eyes showing pity, concern and another emotion I can't place. I have never seen it in someone's eyes before to be able to identify it.

The fish is finally ready, and Ika pulls out one of his many knives, cutting the skin and scales off the fish, handing me a skinned and headless fish on a stick. I have never eaten something so basic in my life, or anything without cutlery. I watch Ika as he holds his fish with both hands on the stick and begins eating. Copying him, I take a small mouthful of fish, careful to ensure that I don't overfill my mouth, and that no juices are caught on my face or dripping onto my clothing.

"Mmmmmmm," I moan, as the first bite passes my lips. I look up and catch Ika's gaze. "This is delicious!" His eyes drop to my mouth as my tongue darts out to lick up the remaining juice. "How does this taste so good? You didn't do anything to it, but cook it on the fire?" I ask, taking another mouthful. Normally the fish I have at the Palace or luncheons are covered in herbs and oils. It still tastes great, but this fire cooked fish by Ika is so much better.

Realising that Ika has not spoken, my eyes flick to him, noticing he is frozen and is staring at me. "What?" I question abruptly "Do I have something on my face?" reaching my hand up to wipe my face.

His head flies back, as if woken from a daydream, shaking his head he finally looks away from me. "Uh, sorry, I was lost in my own head. What did you ask me?"

I giggle softly. "I do that all the time, too. Pull on a thread of thought and find myself lost unravelling it in my own mind. It's how I got lost in the woods, actually." I confess to him, "I was lost in my own thoughts and not paying attention to where Stormy was walking. When I learnt how to ride as a child, I was taught how to tell directions and time by the sun's point in the sky. Once I realised, I was lost, I wasn't able to see the sky anymore, so I couldn't find which direction I needed to head in. Then I found a clearing that was big enough for me to see the sky, and your cabin. And here we are," I say with a small smile. He had kept eating as I spoke, his fish now finished. "So, Ika," I start, "tell me about what you do. You said you don't have any livestock or produce farming, so what do you do in a cabin all alone in the woods?"

"I am a lumberjack and a woodcarver." His voice husky, still not making eye contact with me since... since I moaned? Is that right? He lost himself in his own head staring at me just after I moaned and complimented him on his food. Had I distracted him? I moan again while taking another bite of my fish, testing out to see his reaction. His eyes snap back to my mouth as he watches me chew and swallow. The thought that his man can be as captivated by me as I am by him makes me feel giddy, no matter how stupid it is to want that.

Chapter Twelve

PRINCESS GERTRUDE

"Mhat's a lumberjack?" I ask while a smug grin stretches my face, the fact that my moaning could have an effect on this hulking, amazing specimen of a man, trills me.

"I harvest, carve and transport trees and sell to carpenters for houses, buildings, transport like carriages and wagons, furniture and such." Thankfully, he doesn't sound annoyed at having to explain his profession to me, he must encounter a lot of people who don't know what a lumberjack is, or he has a lot of patience for me. Perhaps he resents that someone who clearly has a good education and upbringing, doesn't know that lumberjacks existed, and he sought to rectify that.

"Are you not too far away from other people in your cabin? Would you not need to be somewhere closer to villages and towns to then sell your wares?"

"I need to be close to the forest. That is where the trees are, where the work is. I make trips into villages throughout the spring, summer and autumn months to sell any wood that I have. My father was a well-known lumberjack in these parts, and many of the townspeople remember that and know who I am. I am often sought out and given orders to fill, rather than having to source someone to purchase what I have already cut and prepared."

"Where does the 'woodcarver' come into the work?"

"It is something I do more for fun and extra money on the side. I need to do an element of carving to prepare the wood for the buyer. Removing bark, branches and such. It then developed into something to fill the nights and winter months. I started when I was thirteen years old, learning how to use a carving knife to make things out of off cuts of wood. I got so good, some of my work was purchased and on display in the galleries of Adaira."

"I saw a few carvings when I visited the gallery. There was a beautiful bust carving, that was you?"

He nods, "Yes that bust was of my mother, I carved it from memory of her face after she passed away when I was seventeen."

No wonder he was gruff and broody sometimes, he has been alone for a long time. Suddenly, an idea hits me. I want art works, and I am going to speak with Mr Smithers about contacting artists, and here one is in front of me.

"Do you do commissions? Would you be able to carve something for me? I don't have any wood carvings in my collection, I would be honoured if you would create something for me. It can be anything you like, I don't much care for the subject. I prefer more imagining why the artist chose subjects, materials and the emotions and thoughts behind artworks. I could pay you." The words rapidly fall out of me, speaking so fast they I barely took a breath. I don't want to beg, but I felt like I was about to start. With a jolt, I realise that I want a physical memory of Ika. I want something to keep a hold of once I return to life as Princess Gertrude, too look back and know that it was real. That he was real, and I was able to be real with him.

"No." He responds flatly. "I have not carved in four years." Sadness radiates off him, as pain crinkles across his face, lost in a memory.

"I am going to take Stormy to the creek for some water," giving him time to compose himself. While Stormy drinks, I pat her down again, ensuring she is comfortable after the long day's travel.

"How did we get here Stormy?" I never thought when I left the Palace this morning that I would end up camping overnight with a lumberjack. I still can't undecide if this is a good thing or not. "At least we got our adventure."

I return to the campsite with Stormy and tie her back up. Turning to face the fire, Ika has placed out the lumpy rolled material I had seen him unpack earlier. "Bedrolls, you sleep in it," Ika explains. I watch him studying my face. Exhausted, I school my expression and sit down on the vacant bedroll, removing my shoes and placing them next to me.

"Good night, Ika," settling down into my bedroll.

He doesn't respond, just sat there staring at the fire. Just as I start to drift into sleep, I thought I heard him mumble, "Too sweet and beautiful for her own good."

Chapter Thirteen

IKA

I sit there staring at her sleeping figure like a creep. How can this woman be so unique and beautiful? Her reaction to me at the stream and the fire puzzles me, drawing me in closer to who this woman is. She is blunt, honest, strange and odd. I have never met anyone like Trudy, and I don't know what to do.

I have not carved anything in years, it has always been an emotional venture for me. After what happened in Adaira, I have not able to bring myself to pick up the tools. Looking at Trudy now, I'm itching to carve the shape of her sleeping form. To enable me to keep a part of her with me after she returned to her life. Trudy probably thought I was crazy, spouting things about mystery Princesses and the cursed forests. It is hard to tell how long she has been missing for. I truly hope that she is able to return to her house and life tomorrow without too many changes. I can tell she thought I have lost my mind; I am happy to let her live in that delusion for now. It will fall soon enough and arguing with her over who is right isn't going to change the outcome of her return.

Giving in, I pick up a large branch from the pile of firewood Trudy had collected earlier and pull my knife out of my boot. To not wake her, I quietly reacquaint myself with the feel of my knife against the wood and begin stripping the wood of its bark. Muscle memory taking over, I lose track of the time as I clean and carve the branch. Allowing my mind to float away, thinking of Trudy arriving on my doorstep this afternoon.

The first thing that assaulted me was her chocolate brown eyes, the same shade as her long hair. They pulled me in, drowning me in their depths. She looked travel worn and exhausted, but those eyes could still scorch me if she tired. I have never had a woman be as direct and demanding of me, she knew what she needed and would not stop until she got it.

My fingers take over as an image comes to life on the wood in my hands. Looking down at the object in my hands, I am shocked my mind has produced such a form. I thought I wanted to carve something for myself, to keep as a memory. Surprisingly, I have carved something for Trudy.

I stand from my bedroll and walk to her saddle. Being careful not to make any noises that would wake Trudy, I place the carving in one of the bags on her saddle. I hope that when she eventually finds the carving, it will bring a smile to her face, even if I am not there to see it. The thought of Trudy having a piece of me, sinks deep into my heart and warms me up. Wishing I could somehow give her more of me. She now has something to remember me and this little adventure by. Gathering all the wood pieces I add them to the fire before returning to my bedroll and bunking down inside. It will be hard to fall asleep tonight, with a beautiful stranger at my side out in the open wilderness. I haven't had a night like this in a long time, and I am starting to think the change in routine might be good for me.

Chapter Fourteen

PRINCESS GERTRUDE

I wake with the sun shining brightly in my eyes. It takes me a moment to remember that I am not in my bed at the Palace but am camping with a near stranger. A handsome, standoffish stranger. Sitting up slowly, I look over to where his bed roll is and find him flat on his back, mouth open and jaw slack, softly snoring. He looks adorable in sleep. All the harshness and stress has left his face, and he looks at peace for the first time since I met him.

Deciding it is a good time for me to go and bathe in the creek I quietly get out of my bedroll and pick up my boots. Grabbing the cake of soap Ika had left out for me on his bag and walking barefoot down to the creek, this time taking the effort to walk slowly and conceal any noise my footsteps could make to stir Ika. I have never bathed in the open before and the thought of it is exhilarating and slightly terrifying. Knowing that Ika is asleep and unlikely to wake up and watch me is even more motivation to go now before he can come looking for me. I strip off quickly and jump into the fresh cold water.

"Ah!" I squeal, slapping my hand over my mouth. The water is freezing, the morning sun doing nothing to heat the rapidly moving stream.

I wash quickly, rushing to get out of the icy water. Letting my hair down from the braid, I wash and finger brush it, and leaving it hanging down my spine to dry out.

"Shit!" I mutter under my breath, realising I forgot something to dry off with. Making the best of the situation, I get out the stream and sit naked on one of the stone boulders at the water's edge, hoping the sun and air would quickly dry me before Ika came looking. The moment I had the sun rays on me without the cold water I started to warm up again. Thankfully, Ika either wasn't awake yet or he didn't bother with coming to look for me.

Mostly dry, I make my way over to my clothing. Pulling on my panties and camisole, before my skirt and jacket, before sitting back on the boulders to put my boots back on. As I put my left foot into my boot, I encounter something soft and squishy. "That's weird," I muse aloud while still trying to get my foot into the boot. Suddenly the squishy thing in the shoe moves, and a sharp intense pain breaks out in my left toes.

I scream at the top of my lungs in pain. Not knowing what to do, I remove my foot from the boot, and out comes a snake. As the snake's head peaks out of the boot, Ika comes running and steps on to the rocky bed.

"What the fuck?" he asks, taking in the scene around him. Me sitting on a boulder, dressed but I had my skirt hiked up around my waist with my panties, unfortunately, on display for him. My right boot is secured on my foot, while my left foot is bleeding, and my left boot is in my hands with a snake coming at me.

"HELP! HELP!" I scream at Ika, "IT BIT ME!"

Ika rushes forward and grabs the snake out of my boot. Holding it securely behind its head he starts to investigate the markings on the snake. With the snake out of my hands, I fix my skirts to cover myself. "What are you doing? KILL IT!" I yell.

"I need to know what type of snake it is first, woman. Stop your screeching. Good news. It's a baby carpet python."

"HOW IS THAT GOOD NEWS, IKA!?" I am still yelling. I can't calm down. My foot is still throbbing in pain.

"It's not venomous. So, while you are hurt, you won't die from the bite. He probably crawled in your shoes last night as somewhere warm to sleep and was woken up when you put your foot on his face." Ika says with a slight smirk on his face, almost distracting me.

"Is this supposed to be amusing? It's somehow my fault that I was bitten by a fucking snake?" Swearing to get my point across.

"It's all good Darlin', no need to get those white panties in a twist." He walks over to where I am still sitting, shoe in hand and wraps his arms around me. He lifts me in one easy swoop, one arm around my shoulders and the other under my legs. I scramble to wrap my arms around his neck quickly, holding on to ensure that I don't fall.

"What are you doing!?" I ask him exasperated.

"What does it look like, I am taking you back to the camp, so I can clean and bind your foot before we set out for today. It's not like you could walk barefoot through the forest with an open wound. You would be opening yourself up to all kinds of infections. Couldn't have you losing any of your pretty toes now could we Darlin'?"

He places me down on my bedroll and walks to his bag. Removing a small pouch, he returns and sits next to me on the bed roll facing me. Placing my left foot in his lap, Ika works in silence, going about cleaning the snake bite with a medicine, and then wrapping it up tightly. Once secure, he places my stocking over my foot and put my boot on for me. It is a strangely intimate task. I have been dressed by servants my whole life but had never felt the way I did with Ika putting a stocking and shoe on my foot.

"All good Darlin', how are you feeling now?"

"Sore, but better. Thank you. How did you know to check what type of snake that was? How did you know what to do?" I ask in amazement.

"I have encountered a lot of snakes in the forest and had to learn what to do when they bite, or how to avoid an attack. Now we can't sit around here all day, we need to head off if we are going to get you home."

"Uh... I hate to ask this of you Ika, but I have never done my own hair before. Would you be able to braid mine so it's out of the way for the walk?"

Surprise showing at my question, Ika just nods and moves to sit behind me. He has a soft and gentle touch, carefully combing through my locks with his fingers and untangling as he braids my hair. Ika hands feel amazing in my hair, and I bite down on my lips trying to contain a hum from contentment at his touch, that might make things awkward.

I feel a lead weight settle in my chest at the thought of going home, and never getting to experience life like this again. In silence, my hair was finished, and remorsefully I help Ika pack up the bed rolls and prepare Stormy for another day's worth of walking.

We leave our campsite behind, and begin our walk resuming the pace and atmosphere of silence from yesterday. If this is the only time that I was going to really be able to be myself around another person, then I want more memories to relive for the rest of my life.

"So, tell me more about you Ika."

"What would you like to know?"

"Anything you feel like sharing. We barely know each other, and I doubt we will see each other again after today. You can tell me anything you would like to and know it wouldn't go anywhere."

"Hmm. Well, you basically know all there is to know about me. I live alone, I am a lumberjack and wood carver. I don't like people's company."

"If you don't like people's company, or strangers, why are you helping me get home?"

"I hardly know. There is something lingering in my mind. It's like a calling, telling me that I must see you home safe. I cannot explain it very well."

He felt a calling to ensure I got home safe? Ika had been a stranger, still is really, and yet he felt responsible for ensuring my safety? My heart swells.

"Thank you," I reply softly. I don't know what else there is to say.

Gruffly, he changes the conversation. "We were much closer to the Palace after our journey and camp yesterday. So, we are about an hour away from the main market now."

So close already? What am I going to tell my family about my overnight trip? How can I tell Ika who I really am? He will find out the moment a guard or servant laid eyes upon me.

We take a break next to a small creek, letting Stormy take a long drink of water and giving ourselves a rest. I am trying to delay having to leave Ika, and I hope he felt the same. I need more from him. I can't explain it, but I feel safe with him. Happy and this contentedness that I cannot put into words.

Catching his eyes, I take a leap and ask, "Ika, why don't you carve anymore? When you speak of it you sound both in pain and longing for the feeling and peace it gave you, why did you stop?"

He looks away from me, that same pained expression from last night on his face. Ika lets out a deep breath and starts speaking quickly, like he is just wanting to get it over with.

"Roughly four years ago, King Kryler set the village of Adaira aflame. He was angry that King Mason had insulted him over his daughter, Gertrude. Things between them were already strained when King Charming married Queen Cinderella, but when Princess Gertrude went missing, King Mason blamed Charming, stating that he had stolen her away to be his mistress. Honestly, the whole situation doesn't make sense to me." Shaking his head, I feel like I have just been punched, "King Kryler retaliated, and not long before his death he burned Adaira. Rumour has it he had just learned that Princess Gertrude had visited there the day she went missing, and wanted to stop any chance King Mason and, then Prince now King Harrison had of tracking her down. King Kryler sent soldiers in the middle of the night, they blocked all doorways and windows, and set everything on fire. There were no survivors. All of my friends, the children, buildings; all gone. I tried to save them, I got there in the end and tried to get someone, anyone out. Since the horror of that day, I have not been able to carve again. Not until I met you." He mutters the end, finally meeting my watery gaze. I cannot not believe this, but I cannot call him a liar either.

"I'm sorry, Ika." I reach out a hand to him in comfort, and he grasps it gently.

Now I really cannot tell him who I am, he will hate me. If what he said was really true, he had lost everything because of me.

We spend a few moments in silence, holding hands in comfort. Gently Ika withdrew his hand from mine and starts preparing for us to continue walking again. I am looking forward to a hot bath tonight, I had aches and pains from so much walking.

"We are close now Ika, you can head home now if you like. I can take it from here." I tell him, keeping my emotions from my voice. How could one day and a few small moments have such a substantial impact on me? The idea of being separated from him is repulsive to me, but it needs to happen. He will hate me when he realises who I am, which will happen the moment we get to the main market.

"Not gonna happen, Darlin'. I told you I'd see you home, and that's what I am going to do."

I take Stormy's reins for our last leg of the journey. We continue in our previous style, not speaking and I spend the walk overthinking instead. It keeps hitting me that I don't want to leave Ika. I wish I could have just stayed in the woods with him, that I could have been selfish for once in my life and done what I wanted. Yet, I knew my duty to my Kingdom. I knew I needed to return to the Palace. Maybe once I had returned, we could maintain contact. Nothing said I never had to see him again, he would need to know who I am though; and as much as it was going to hurt him, I need to be the one to tell him before he finds out for himself.

Looking up from my hands, which were ringing Stormy's reins, "Ika, I need to tell you something!" I called out to him, noticing the entrance to the Palace. No, we couldn't be here already!

He looks back at me, "Yes, Darlin'?" I open my mouth to respond, as a Palace guard walks around the gate and sees us.

"Princess Gertrude! You have returned!" Turning to another guard, he starts issuing orders, "Call the King, he must be told at once!" He turns back to me "Come Princess. George here will take Stormy to the stables, and I will escort you inside to the King."

My eyes did not leave Ika's face as the guard spoke. I can see all the emotions play across his face as the guards' words sink in. Before I can speak with Ika or tell him anything, I am manhandled away from Stormy and ushered inside the Palace. With a final glance over my shoulder, I see another guard talking to Ika.

Chapter Fifteen

IKA

*P*rincess Gertrude. Not Trudy. How stupid could I have been to trust her?

"Sir, who are you?" A guard asks, pulling me from my thoughts.

"Ika." I clip out. Turning to the market, I need to gather more supplies before I start heading home. As it hit me that Stormy was being led away with my bag, the guard grabbed my arm, halting my retreat.

"Sir, you will be required to see the King. Either you can go inside willingly, or I can restrain you and take you in by force. What do you choose?"

Perfect. So not only have I been escorting a Princess home for the last day, but now I had to see her idiot King of a brother and probably face the death sentence because she has been missing for four years, and I am the one who brought her home. It never crossed my mind that she could have been the Princess. She looked only eighteen and the Princess would be verging on twenty-two, and she was dressed so nicely. If you had been missing for four years would you not be somewhat scrappy? My stomach twists into knots, how could I be such an idiot? She was trapped in the Silent Wood all that time. She wouldn't have aged at all. How could I have not realised it sooner?

My unique, strange, beautiful Trudy, the woman I have an overwhelming urge to protect, who I am starting to care for, is the Princess Gertrude of Daes.

Before the guard can force me to do anything, I walk down the pathway to the Palace, mentally preparing myself for what could be one of the worst meetings in my life.

Chapter Sixteen

PRINCESS GERTRUDE

*E*scorted to the Throne Room, I enter to find my brother sitting on the throne, looking older than had last at dinner the night. How can he have aged so much in two days?

"Harrison, what is going on? What is all the fuss over, I have been gone just over twenty-four hours. Where is Father?"

Shock colours Harrison's expression as he sits there staring at me.

"You dare to speak to me in such a way?!" Harrison barks. What is he getting at? We always speak to each other this way. He is the Crown Prince of this Kingdom, and my older brother. He has always demanded my respect and submission to him, as my superior, but we are still informal most of the time.

"I am sorry Harrison, but I do not understand what is going on? Where is Mother and Father?" I ask softly, bowing my head; trying to appease him however I can. He is obviously in one of his moods today.

"Where are Mother and Father?! Where have you been?! You have been missing for four years Gertrude, and the first words out of your mouth aren't explaining where you were, but are instead making demands of your King?"

"K-K-King?" I stutter. Ika hadn't been right, had he? Surely, I haven't actually been gone for four years. "I swear Harrison, I only left yesterday morning. I rode out to Adaira to look at the galleries and buy art, then I got lost in the woods. I managed to find a cabin and made my way back with the assistance of Ika." Who I will never see again, and I will never get to explain to him who I am.

"That was four years ago Gertrude, I am King now. Not just Harrison to you anymore." His voice is so cold, heartless. This isn't the Harrison I knew. The Harrison I knew is rude, but nothing like this. I am so lost, what is happening?

"I don't understand. Where is Father?"

"He died looking for you. Three years ago. Mother died a month before him, due to the stress and sadness of a runaway daughter. So, tell me, why have you come back now? After all these years? Did King Charming finally get bored with you?"

"She was trapped in the Silent Wood, Your Majesty." Ika's gravelly voice cuts through the Throne Room. Turning towards his voice, I watch as he is escorted in by a guard. Shaking off the guards hold; he bows to Harrison. Ika doesn't look in my direction and I cannot get a read on his emotions. How does he feel about me being a Princess? Or about me not being honest with him about who I am?

Harrison's eyes flick between us, "Convenient." Sitting further back in the throne, Harrison continues, "How did you find your way into the Silent Wood, Gertrude?"

"I don't know, I was heading home from Adaira and then found myself on his doorstep." Indicating Ika, "This whole talk of a cursed wood is absurd, even as a prank from you Harrison. I know you are cruel, but not like this. Where are Mother and Father? This isn't funny."

"I already told you. They are dead, they died while looking for you. Everyone thought King Charming stole you and either kept you as his whore or killed you. No one has seen you for four years Gertrude, what do you think that does to a Kingdom when their Princess just disappears?"

"They didn't even care about me! They all forgot about me. They forgot my birthdays and didn't bother with my existence unless it was for a marriage of convenience or beneficial for them! And you are trying to make me think they died over me, purely because I was no longer their burden?"

"I tried telling her on our journey, Your Majesty." Ika speaks harshly, breaking into our conversation. Harrison looks taken aback, like he has forgotten Ika was in the room. I hadn't though, all the cells in my body are alert and aware of his presence. "I have told Tru-Princess Gertrude; the Silent Wood was cursed and that she had likely been held captive for years. I did not know she is Princess Gertrude at the time and did not make the connection for her disappearance." I flinch as he says my name.

Harrison turns back to me, "Gertrude, you left here four years ago. I will keep saying it until it sinks in. You have been missing for four years." Turning back to Ika, Harrison asks, "Why did you bring her here? Were you ordered to deliver her from King Charming?"

I was starting to get very frustrated with my brother. "I found him at his house when I was lost. Prince, King or whatever you want to call him Charming, wasn't holding me captive. Have you gone crazy? He never wanted me, you knew that and constantly shoved it in my face! Why would you think he had stolen me in the bright of day a mere three months after he got married? Ika has nothing to do with this. If you two are right, then I was trapped for four years. I was not held captive by anyone other than the Silent Wood. Which I didn't even know existed!"

"He is an idiot. You and I both know it was stupid of him to marry Cinderella over you. Why would you know it existed? You were raised to live in another Kingdom, you were never taught about your own." Harrison exclaims. He sounds jealous, that couldn't be right. Why would he be jealous of me? "Why would you need to learn about places you should never have encountered? You never left this Palace unaccompanied, or have travelled so far alone, so it shouldn't have been an issue. What were you thinking, Gertrude? You just woke up one day and left the Palace. Alone. No note or explanation, just gone and you turn up four years later? Who's to say you were not brainwashed against us? Or are a secret spy for Charming. You always loved him, I wouldn't be surprised if you ran away to sign up as his whore and only come back now because it is convenient for you."

I roll my eyes and cut him off, "You are crazy. I never loved him. I loved the idea of getting the fuck out of this Palace!" I turn from the surprise on Harrison's face and storm from the room, walking towards my bedroom. I could feel a guard following me, tracking my movements to report back to the "King". Instead of going straight to my bedroom I detour to the library. I need to check what Harrison and Ika were saying and prove that I haven't been missing for four years. IKA! I'd left him in the Throne Room alone with Harrison! I rush back to the throne room, entering to see Ika being restrained between two guards.

"What are you doing?" I demand Harrison, as I feel two guards grab a hold of me too. "Let me go!"

"I am going to hold you both until I can ensure that you are not out to destroy this Kingdom."

With rough hands holding my arms, we shuffle down the hallway and into a chamber. The guards let me go, releasing me to fall onto the stone floor. Scrambling to get my feet underneath me and stand up, I hear them slam the door shut.

"NO!" I rush to the door and try to open it, pulling the handle and slamming my palm into the door.

"You can't do this to me! I am not a prisoner!" I scream, "I can't be a prisoner, not again." My voice breaks on a sob, as I push my back against the door and slid to the ground.

I was locked in a room again. I finally had freedom. Four years of glorious freedom and I didn't even know it.

Chapter Seventeen

IKA

I am locked in a jail cell. A fucking cell. I had heard stories about how crazy King Harrison was, but I assumed they were overstated by idiots.

When I was twelve, I told myself that I would never come back. After what the King and Queen did to my family, I had sworn I wouldn't come anywhere near their Palace. Now I find myself trapped inside a cell, for escorting the Princess back here?

What did I even say yes for? I scoff at my own thoughts. I can't kid myself. I know I did it because I was struck dumb by Tru – Princess Gertrude. I have never met anyone who equals her fiery personality. I have known she is special from the moment I laid eyes on her, special enough to be a Queen apparently.

I pace my cell while working through my thoughts. This wasn't intentional for her. She didn't even believe she has been missing for four years, so this wasn't a trap for me. I don't think she was even aware of who I am, Tru – Princess Gertrude probably didn't remember me from when we lived here. I can't stop stumbling over her name. I would not have thought she is a Princess from how she treated me and behaved. Trudy is so kind and caring. She listened to me like she was interested in what I had to say.

I hear doors slam, and sobbing comes from the wall next to me. Had King Harrison thrown Trudy in a cell, too? I lean against the wall connecting me with her cell and slide down to sit on the floor with my back against the wall, listening to her cries.

"I'm here, Darlin'. You aren't alone." That gut feeling, I can't understand overcomes me again, I need to reassure her. Need her to know that I am here, that she isn't alone and that I don't care that she is a Princess.

Chapter Eighteen

PRINCESS GERTRUDE

*M*y head snaps up at the sound of his voice.

"Ika?"

"I'm here, Trudy." I crawl towards his voice, needing to be closer to him.

My voice breaks with my sobs, "I-I-I am so sorry, Ika. S-s-sorry I made you walk here. Sorry you got arrested. Sorry I didn't tell you who I am. Th-thi-this is all my fault."

"Uh, yeah. *Princess?*" he stretches out the word, turning it into a question. "Why didn't you tell me who you are?"

I calm myself, taking deep breaths and really thinking about how I wanted to answer that.

"At first, I didn't want anyone to know who I was. I was enjoying the freedom of just being me for the day, you kn-know?" I hiccup, "Then, you started talking all about the Mystery Princess, and you knew Charming left me for her. I didn't want you to see me as inferior to her, I wanted you to get to know me before you could judge me based on a story. I could be free and alive with you, Ika. I have not felt able to be myself since I was ten years old. I was betrayed and I haven't allowed myself to be who I am since, I needed to protect myself." I cannot stop talking now it has started spewing out of me. If we are going to be locked up, possibly forever, I want him to know everything. "It was my fault, always my fault. I have ruined lives, ruined villages."

I start sobbing again, knowing that Ika will be disgusted with me now and I hate myself for caring that he would. He will see the selfish Princess bitch that everyone sees. Crying until my sobbing eased and my throat was raw. It feels like hours have passed, but I am all dried out now. Ika has not spoken at all in that time.

"Well? Say something."

"That was a lot of information to take in, Darlin'. I needed time to sort through it all, and I wanted you to have time to process your own feelings. I'm trying to not be offended that you didn't trust me with who you were, and to understand why you felt you needed to keep it to yourself. I have so many questions. What do you mean that everything is your fault? How have you ruined things, with your own hands?"

"Well no, everything happened because of me. Adaira was lost because I went there. I let myself get manipulated by Evalyn. I told her my secrets because I thought she was my friend. I should have known better, she turned on me and reported everything back to my Mother. She sabotaged everything to get to me. My fault."

"And how is that your fault, Darlin'? This sounds like other people's actions that you are taking the blame for. You did not make them act this way, you did not force King Kryler to burn Adaira, that was his decision. And Evalyn, whoever the fuck that is, made the choice to betray you. The outcome is hers to own, not yours."

I stand and start pacing, "You don't get it. A boy and his father lost their job, their livelihood, everything, because of me. I told Evalyn I liked the grounds' boy when I was ten years old. That same day my mother had them escorted from the grounds, so I wouldn't get distracted from my *goal*: to marry Charming. Look how well that turned out for me, he didn't marry me! I don't know what happened to the boy and his family. I never even knew his name, and I ruined their lives."

Ika doesn't respond and I remain silent, giving him the time to think. I continue pacing and look around my cell now that I have calmed down. It holds nothing to pull my attention. It is composed of four grey stone walls, a small window set high in the wall. Nothing is in the room except a bucket and a pile of straw in a corner which I think is meant to be a bed. There are small holes in the wall between my cell and Ika's.

"Y-you do know what happened to the boy, Darlin'." He finally chokes out, drawing me back to the wall.

"No, I don't. I just told you that."

"I-I'm that boy, Trudy. I worked here with my father, Oscar, until I was 12 years old, when we were forced to leave. Are you saying that we had to leave because you told this Evalyn, what, that you liked me?"

Ika. Ika is the green-eyed boy. I pull up the memory of the green-eyed boy and put his face next to Ika's in my mind.

"Oh Shit!" I stumble and fell to the floor. Ika is the green-eyed boy. I can see the same eyes, same smile. "Oh, Ika. Oh my. Holy fucking balls."

He breaks out in laughter, guffawing unlike I have ever heard from him.

"Oh Trudy, Darlin'. There is never a dull moment with you is there? *'Holy fucking balls,'*" he mimics, still laughing as he continues, "Clearly, I am fine, Darlin'. I never even thought you were the reason behind why we left. I had always blamed your folks. Darlin', to be honest with you, it was a blessing in disguise. Because we left the Palace, my folks got to spend more time together before they passed. My mum and dad both got to pass happy, and knowing that we had those good, happy years together. If we hadn't left, I never would have had the time to find carving and experience that joy in my life."

"Y-you don't hate me?" I ask him tentatively, mulling over his words.

"Nah, Darlin'. I don't know why, the last few years I have
hated the idea of even coming back to the heart of the Kingdom. But, as I told you at our camp, there is something about
you that speaks to me; calls me to be here with you, to trust and
help you." Shaking my head, I turn to lean my back against the
wall between us as he continues, "I can't believe you are that
little girl. You used to wear your hair in these little plaits and had
picnics with that governess woman before going off to see your
horse. Of course," I hear a slapping noise, "that's Stormy,
isn't it?"

"Did you just hit something?"

"Uh, yeah. I hit myself in the face..." shame coating his voice
as it trails off.

"Why?"

"Seriously, Trudy? Cause I'm an idiot! I should have used my
brain and realised all this information sooner. Put two and two
together and realise that you had been missing for the same
amount as time as the Princess, because you are the missing
Princess."

"How can you say you are an idiot; I didn't realise either. Are
you calling me stupid now too?"

"Well, no. I wouldn't insult you like that. You're a Princess
for Pete's sake, why would I insult you?"

"NO!" I scream, "No, no, no! To you I am not a Princess,
Ika. I never wanted you to see me as a Princess - that's the
reason I kept that information from you. Why would I want you
to treat me differently? All my life, everyone has treated me like
I am either a nuisance, an arrangement for them, or like I am
superior to them because of my fickle bloodline. I don't want it!
Can't you see I just want to be normal? Being with you was the
first time in my life that I have ever gotten to be normal. Please
don't see me as a Princess now." I plead with him.

"Okay, Trudy. Okay."

"Okay?"

"Yeah, Darlin'. Okay."

"I'm sorry I yelled," I say with a sigh, "Thank you."

"So, Darlin', what are we going to do?"

"What do you mean?"

"I mean are we going to sit here and wait for that idiot brother of yours to come to his senses, or are we going to escape?"

"Escape? Why? What would we do? Run into Charming's Kingdom?" I laugh, "Spend the rest of our lives on the run, being hunted by my brother? You don't deserve to be lumped in with me, and where would I even live? The only home I have ever known is this Palace. The only people I have ever known live here too. I don't have any practical skills, I cannot go and get a job as a handmaid or ladies' maid, I don't know how to do anything. What do you suggest I do, if not sit here and wait?"

"Well, Darlin'. We could spend our lives together. You could come and live with me in the woods, for one."

I gasp, choking on my breath, I utter, "L-l-live with you? Why would you want that?"

"To be honest with you, on our journey here the thought of leaving you and being without you tore at me. I cannot put into words what I am feeling for you right now, but I would like the chance to figure it out. I can also think of several reasons I would want you around, Darlin'. Don't worry, I can teach you everything you need to know." I can hear the play on his words, hinting to what exactly he wants to teach me.

"How would you propose we get out of here, Ika? We are locked in a cell!"

Chapter Nineteen

KING HARRISON

*W*hy would he send her back? She is what most men would want; beautiful, wealthy, with a powerful family; and he sent her away? Then again, Charming has always been an idiot. He married a peasant over Gertrude, for fucks sake. Father was always so adamant that she was stolen, taken and abused. Yet here she appears, four years later, not looking a day older than the last time I saw her.

The first time I met up with Ambrose after Gertrude went missing, he tried convincing me that his family hadn't taken her. I had questioned him and didn't trust his word. I haven't spoken to him since, although that also has something to do with Evalyn and her manipulative ways.

Could this Ika fellow be right? Could Gertrude have simply been lost in the woods for four years, until she found him? If that is to be believed, she is lucky to find such a man kind enough to bring her home.

Since the guards locked them up two hours ago, I have been pacing my Throne Room trying to figure out what to do with the situation. The guards were under orders to not be gossiping idiots, so I knew no one else in the court or Kingdom knew of her return. Now that she is back, what does it mean? There is no way I can issue an apology to King Charming and Queen Cinderella. We have not spoken since the fire of Adaira. It has been hard not being able to reach out, Ambrose and Charming were my closest friends. While we are at odds with their Kingdom, reconnecting with Ambrose is both my deepest desire and what scares me the most. I don't know how to resolve things with Ambrose, we had argued over Gertrude's disappearance, but I would be kidding myself if I said there weren't other differences that would need to be sorted out before we could even discuss moving forward.

Evalyn has the ability to always appear at the worst possible moment. Cutting off my stride mid-pace, she begins speaking in a sultry tone. "My King, what troubles you so? Is there anything I can do to help you?"

"Not today, Evalyn. There is nothing for which I require your assistance." Dismissing her, I turn and continued pacing.

Evalyn has been trying to get me into her bed for the last three years. She is fifteen years older than me and has known me since she began to care for Gertrude, when I was ten. After Gertrude went missing, I asked Ambrose to meet me in our Garden so I could discuss Father's accusations with him, Evalyn interrupted a heated argument we were having and found out more information than she had a right too. Ever since, she has held it over my head to manipulate me. At her demand, I have let her stay on in the Castle as an attempt to appease her, but her contentment is starting to wane. I would need to start thinking of other ways I could handle her, and soon.

"Actually Evalyn, I have a question for you."

"You can ask me anything, Your Majesty."

"Why did Gertrude hate you?" I had a good idea after Evalyn's behaviour toward me over the last few years, but I want to be sure.

"Where has this come from, Your Majesty?"

"Call it curiosity. You never speak of her, you cared for her for eleven years before her disappearance. Many would assume you as friends after so long caring for her. So please tell me, why did she hate you?"

"I do not know what you mean, My King." Her shrill voice echoes around the room, "We were close friends."

"When she was younger, that may have been so. However, she was increasingly cold towards you, and everyone really, before she went missing. Do you think she might have run away? Father always dismissed the idea, he was so hell-bent on the idea that Charming had stolen her, but something is churning my gut. I feel like I am missing something."

I watch as Evalyn's face slowly twisted from her real smile, to her fake smile. I have grown familiar with the difference.

"I don't know what you mean, Your Majesty. That's just who she was, an ungrateful bitch of a girl. Cold to everyone, even you if I remember correctly. She had the world at her fingertips, and yet she wanted a dirty farm-boy. Her head was always in the clouds believing in fairy tales and her stories. I just brought her back to reality."

Evalyn's eyes widen, and I can tell she didn't mean to give that much away.

"Well, well, Evalyn. Looks like I am not the first person you have manipulated. You should leave me now. I have other matters I must attend to."

Sitting on my Throne, I watch her saunter her way out of the room. I'm sure she thought it was sexy and would grasp my attention. Out of everyone, she should know better after what she heard and witnessed.

I think back to who Gertrude was when we were children, how she was so carefree and happy. Something must have happened to turn her into someone who was so cold, and different. Maybe Ika was right, maybe Gertrude was never stollen, instead she was a woman who wanted to escape and got lost on the way.

Chapter Twenty

IKA

"We should rest for now and see what happens with King Idiot, alright Darlin'? We had a few big days walking here, and we could use some time to gather our strength, before we try doing anything too daring."

"Okay, Ika. I haven't done anything like this before. Last time I left, I just walked straight out the doors before anyone was awake, I didn't have to put much effort into it." Her voice is strained after the emotion and physical exertion the last few days.

"I think I'll just have a quick nap, okay?"

"Okay Darlin'. I'll be right here," I joke with small chuckle.

"Ugh!" she groans, and I can picture her rolling her eyes at me.

Falling silent to let her sleep, I sit thinking about Trudy, her reactions to me, to the word Princess, and the possibility of staying here are revealing. Turning over the last few hours of conversation in my mind, I remember her first words after she was deposited in the cell.

'I can't be a prisoner, not again.' At first, I had thought she meant her time in the Silent Wood. After our conversation, I am beginning to think it is actually about her time in the Palace.

This woman has had me tied up in knots from the moment I met her on my doorstep. Was that really only yesterday? That couldn't be right. I feel as though I have known Trudy forever. So long that my heart reaches out to her and wants to comfort her when she is in pain. I had seen her around the gardens when we were children, and she was such a sprightly little thing, always wearing a smile so wide, it brightened my entire day even from a distance. Just like it has for the last day, getting to be close to her and get to know her; it has been the best day of my life. Even ending up here in a cell.

I need to get her out of here and keep her safe with me. I know now, she belongs with me. Maybe Ma or Pa are looking down on us and decided to send her into my path for help, to heal me and herself. I know that it will take time for us both to reconcile ourselves with our pasts, yet I know it would be worth it. I can see now what has been speaking to me this whole time, what is calling me to be here with Trudy; it is my soul reaching out for its mate.

Footsteps walking down the hallway jolts me out of my thoughts. The mechanical sounds of Trudy's door being unlocked echo off the stone walls, and I hear someone enter her cell. They gasp and place something on the ground, soft tentative footsteps edging into the room. Trudy hadn't stirred and I am grateful, she needs the rest.

"Please don't wake her," I speak softly to the new arrival, "She has had a long couple of days and needs the break."

The shuffling footsteps retreat into the hall, locking Trudy's door and move to mine. I hold my breath as the door to my cell is opens, and a small petite woman walks inside. From her outfit I can tell that she is a servant here at the Palace. She has olive skin, and black hair as dark as night, I cannot make out more of her features due to the lack of lighting in the cell.

"Who are you? Do you know the Princess?" she asks in a rushed whisper.

"I'm Ika. I met her the yesterday and brought her home." I reply equally quiet, "Although, now I wish I hadn't."

"Why would you bring her back to such an awful place? She was miserable and hated it here."

"You knew Trudy, when she was here?"

"I was one of her maids. Since she left, I have been looking after that horrendous Evalyn." She shakes her head, her disgust apparent across her features.

"Look, what's your name?"

"Mabel."

"Okay, Mabel, we were arrested on our way back into the main market; King Harrison is under the delusion that Trudy could be a spy for Charming." She scoffs, "I need to get her out of here before he can do anything stupid. Can you get Stormy from the stables, and meet us in the gardens? She should have my bag with her, load them on her and bring her, okay?" The stable hand should have fixed her shoe by now, and we can both ride her home. If not, we can walk, it won't be the worst. We have done it before, after all.

"Can you do that for me, Mabel? For Trudy?" I ask again, as Mabel hasn't replied.

Mabel looks me dead in the eye, and I can tell she is assessing me. She is trying to determine if I am serious about keeping Trudy safe and away from here. Mabel just got better in my opinion, she cared about my Darlin' and is willing to do what is best for her.

"Okay, you will need time to get out of the cells and a distraction. I will ensure the guards are away from this hallway between 11 and midnight to allow you time to get out. Tell Trudy to go to her favourite spot in the Garden. I will be waiting there."

With that she sets down a tray of food that I hadn't noticed before, turns and rushes from the room.

Chapter Twenty-One

PRINCESS GERTRUDE

*W*aking in a dark cold room huddled on a pile of straw, it takes me a moment to remember that I was imprisoned in the Palace. Surely, the last few days have been a dream. I would wake soon to realise that it was actually my birthday, or the morning of Charming's Birthday Ball.

I groan, rolling over. A nap on straw following a night on the forest floor is not as comfortable as my cushion covered bed.

"Trudy, Darlin', you awake?" Ika softly asks from the wall between our cells.

"Mmm," I reply as eloquently as possible after a deep sleep.

"Just wanted to make sure you weren't talking in your sleep again."

"What?" Jolting up, "No! What did I say?"

"Just that you thought I was handsome and moaned my name a few times." He says with a laugh.

"I did not!"

"Yeah, you did Darlin'. It's okay, if I had slept, I am sure I would have dreamed of making you moan, too."

Shockwaves course though me; I hadn't expected him to say that. I have been captivated by him from the moment I first met him on his doorstep; I had not considered he would return the attraction.

"You want to make me moan?" I squeak out.

"Yes, Darlin'. I want to hear you moan my name in ecstasy. To see you writhe beneath me as I make you feel better than you have ever imagined, but this wall is in the way, and a cell is no place for that."

"Uh, I don't know what to say to that, Ika."

"For now, how about we talk about us getting out of here. You should have a tray inside your cell somewhere. Mabel brought you some food."

"Mabel was here?"

"Yes, she was here. She is going to help us to escape."

"I find it hard to believe that she would want to help me. After Evalyn betrayed my confidence regarding you, I kept everyone at a distance. I didn't want them to be hurt like you and your family, or to be used against me. I pretended I didn't know any of their names, Mabel and Savannah were my two lady's maids, but I never showed them that I knew, or that I cared. I couldn't leave myself open to that."

For someone who kept everyone at a distance, it is not lost on me the oddity of suddenly trusting a strange man like Ika with everything. There is something about him that just makes me feel safe, makes me feel like I am finally home. Actually home, not this lonely Palace that has never truly been a home to me.

"Darlin', you don't have to justify to me what you needed to do to survive. I appreciate you telling me what happened, but, don't ever think that I will judge you for anything you tell me. Anyway, Mabel is going to meet us in the gardens at your favourite spot in about an hour, so eat up that food, and we can start to head out."

The tray holds a goblet of water, a roll, and a chunk of cured meats and cheese. Picking up the roll, I start pulling it to pieces, alternating bites of meat and cheese with a chunk of bread.

"How are we to get out of the cell, Ika? You failed to mention how we are actually going to get to the gardens." I ask in between mouthfuls.

"The guards your brother employs are a bit on the dull side, Darlin'. Not only have they not checked on us for hours, they did not check me for my weapons before we were locked up. I have a knife in my boot that we are going to use to get through the door."

"How? Break through many doors before?"

"Only when I have to, like when my Darlin' needs me." I can picture his sensual smile; winking at me as he spoke.

"Do you enjoy making me uncomfortable?"

"Yes, I enjoy your responses I can get out of you."

I roll my eyes. Of course, he does, which only means he will keep going until he got a reaction he likes. Setting the empty goblet down after I finished eating, I hear Ika moving about his cell. Then a squeal of metal on metal, followed closely by another squeal, rings through the room.

"Trudy, can you feel against the wall and find the hole closest to my voice. I want to make sure you are there before I put the knife through."

I run my hands along the cobblestone wall and find a gap.

"I'm here, Ika." He slides the blade through, handle first to ensure that I will not cut myself. "Okay, I have it. Now what do I do with it?"

"I'll talk you through this Trudy. It's not going to be too difficult; you'll just need to use your muscles. Walk over to the door and I need you to locate the hinges. One will be just above your head and the other around your ankles. Start with the one on the bottom, at the top of the hinge you will find the head of a pin, get the blade in between the hinge and the head, and then start pulling it upwards."

It takes me a moment and I have to strain all my muscles, but finally the pin slides up through the hinge, then clatters to the floor.

"Good work, Darlin'. How are you going?"

"I'm okay, Ika. Now what do I do?"

"Repeat the same with the hinge above your head. You may need to angle the blade differently to work with your height."

Finding the hinge, I position the knife, pushing until the pin slides out. Huffing and shaking my arms out, I am alarmed when the door suddenly opens. I tense, not sure what is going to happen if we are caught, but relax the moment, I realise it is Ika.

With his trademark smirk, he walks to me and cups my face with both of his hands. "Look at you, Darlin'. Learning new things and breaking out of a cell like the badass Princess you are."

I smile softly at him, proud of myself that I'd been able to open the door.

"As much as I want to devour you, we need to get out of here now before we get caught."

His words catch me by surprise. He wanted to devour me? Me? My tongue darts out to wet my suddenly dry lips and I know he is going to kiss me. I will have my first kiss with the lumberjack, the green-eyed boy, my Ika the man I have always dreamed of. Ika groans, head hanging back he lets go of my face and grabs my hand, reclaiming the knife and placing it back inside his boot, before pulling me towards the door.

"You lived here for eighteen years; you know how to get to the gardens from here?"

"Yes, that way." I indicate down the corridor, and we set off with quick and silent footsteps.

We don't see any guards, for which I am grateful. I'm not sure what Ika's plan is if we do encounter anyone. We make our way down the hall, along a servant's passage, and up the stairs to the ground floor. We are close to the kitchens now. I don't want to risk running into any of the servants, so I turn us away. We sneak past the library and the formal sitting room until finally, we reach the south entrance to the gardens.

"Do you not find it strange, that we have encountered no-one at all?" I ask Ika. "Usually there are guards all along this floor."

"Mabel said she would distract the guards from the hallway in the cell to allow us to get out. She could have ensured that there were none here either."

We walk into the garden and I welcome the familiarity. Glad I get to experience my sanctuary with Ika.

"It hasn't changed," Ika mutters under his breath. I squeeze his hand gently, and lead him towards my favourite spot, where we are to meet Mabel. I'm not sure if she really knew my favourite part of the gardens, but either way we need to keep moving.

We walk in silence, until we reach the old oak tree. It is hard to fathom that for me, it has only been two days since I stood here, but for the tree it has been four years. Mabel sits with Stormy tied up to a nearby tree, grazing.

"Princess Gertrude," Mabel begins, curtsying to me, "I am glad you are okay. I am sorry this has happened to you, and that I could not stop it."

"I understand Mabel, it's okay. There is only so much we can do in any situation; I am glad you are here now to help us. Thank you for bringing Stormy, you know what she means to me."

Mabel stands silent for a moment, watching us. "Anything for you, Your Highness." She curtsies again as we walk to Stormy, untie her and prepare to leave.

"Stay safe, Mabel. Thank you for your help, but don't let on that you helped us, and sound the alarm if you need to. I can't bear the thought of you being hurt because you helped us. Did you want to come with us? That way I can ensure you are safe. Please? Please come with us, Mabel?" I beg, how can I leave her to face Harrison and Evalyn's wrath alone?

"I cannot, Princess. I am needed here by my family. I will keep an eye on things here and try and stop anything in its tracks if I can. You must go now; you are running out of time before they notice."

Ika breaks into our conversation, "Thank you again, Mabel."

"Yes, Thank you." I offer.

Ika allows me to mount Stormy first, so I can shuffle forward and give him space to sit behind me. Once Ika is seated, I lean down and spoke with Stormy.

"Stormy, do you want to see how fast you can go? I know it will be a heavy load, but it's only for now, until we get far enough away." I lean back and feel Ika's warm hands wrap around my waist, pulling me back to be flush against his body as we set off at a gallop. Tingles shoot through my body, fizzing along from the edges of our touching bodies, radiating through me and burning me up inside. Being this close to Ika is sweet form of torture.

Chapter Twenty-Two

IKA

*T*he length of her body presses against me. My hands can feel every pant, every movement as she shifts about in the saddle. Her perfect round ass is pressed right against my cock, every shift and bump making me grow harder.

It takes everything in me to not cup her breasts or her pussy and feel her grind against me. I know she is innocent, and no matter how badly I crave her body, I want the first time she feels my touch to be special.

We ride Stormy in silence, still on edge from our escape, until we get to the campsite we stayed at on our journey to the Palace. I am surprised we were able to pull it off and get away so easily. Arriving in the clearing, I dismount from Stormy first and quickly adjust myself in my pants. Helping Trudy to get down, I remove Stormy's saddle and bags. Glad Mabel had been able to get them for us. Our journey home will be quicker now that we can ride, but Stormy still needs breaks, especially with a double load. Right now, I need space to regroup myself and settle my erection.

"I'm gonna go take a minute, Darlin', take Stormy to get a drink and settle her. Can you unload the bedrolls? Might catch a nap here before we travel the rest of the way home."

A small smile breaks out across her face, "Okay Ika."

She is so sweet. I take Stormy down to the creek bed, wash my hands and my face, and start to refill our water skins while she drinks. After they were full, I grasp a nearby stick, and sharpen one side to a spear while waiting for Stormy to drink her fill. I will need to catch some fish, but it is too dark now, with sunrise still being a couple hours out.

I re-enter the clearing to see my Darlin' cross-legged on her bed roll, eyes closed with the most serene and peaceful expression on her face. As quietly as possible, I walk Stormy over to a tree and tie her up, giving her plenty of space to graze freely and went to sit on my own bedroll. Trudy's eyes open, and she meets my gaze, her smile stretching across her face.

"You have the most beautiful smile." I blurt out, unable to hold the compliment in. She blushes and tucks her chin, cutting off our eye contact.

"Thank you."

I was beginning to learn there is a lot of range to my Darlin's emotions. Trudy can be shy and timid, yet also fierce and stubborn. I am enjoying getting to know her better.

"Now, can I know what made you smile like that?"

"I thought it was obvious," she replies, those deep chocolate eyes sweeping over me. Ah, there is that fierceness I had seen earlier.

"Not to me, Darlin'."

She giggles and sighs, "You, Ika, this whole thing. It hit me when you said 'home'. I will have a home now. I have freedom. I have never felt so calm and at peace in my entire life, and it's all because of you. If I hadn't found you, Ika, I don't know what would have become of me. Not only within the Silent Wood, but within my own life and timeline. Do you believe in fate?"

"I do, yes. I believe that everything happens for a reason. That we are not dealt more cards than we know how to handle, and when we are dealt a difficult hand, we receive assistance when called upon."

"I think you are my fate, Ika. These last few days with you have been magical." She looks down to an item in her hands, "I found this in the saddle bag."

"Yeah, uh, last night when you were sleeping, I started carving it. It's not detailed or nothing, just a basic carving."

"So humble Ika. It's Stormy, isn't it? It's beautiful. I am confused though, you said you didn't carve anymore, and that I couldn't persuade you to carve anything for me."

"I wasn't planning on it, Darlin'. Not until I sat here and watched you sleep so peacefully, that's when I realised, I wanted to have a piece of you to remember our time together. I took a piece of the firewood you had collected and let my hands flow until an image started to form in the wood. When I finished and realised that it was Stormy, I knew it was meant for you, not for me to keep."

"I love it. Thank you."

"You're welcome, Darlin'." I wink and smirk at her. "We can display it in our home."

"You are serious about wanting to live with me?"

"Serious, Darlin', if you want to live with me. If you don't, I will help you find somewhere safe; but I believe you are my fate too. If it weren't for you starting a series of events, my family wouldn't have had those last amazing years together. Speaking of, we never really addressed the whole you having a crush on me when we were kid's thing. So, you liked the grounds' boy, did you?"

Her beautiful face tinging a bright pink, she stammers, "I-I did, yes."

"Did? You don't still? After the way, your eyes heated up when you saw me in the creek, I thought you might still want me now." She drops my gaze and looking ashamed. Now I can't be having that. I stand and walk over to my Darlin', crouch in front of her, hooking my finger under her chin and tilting her face back to meet my gaze.

"There's nothing to be ashamed about, Darlin'. I want you

too." Trudy's eyes widen at my declaration, and I can feel her pulse speed up beneath my fingertips as they brush against her throat.

"If you want me, why don't you kiss me? Why didn't you kiss me in the cell? You pulled back, Ika."

"Don't confuse me wanting to do right by you, and for it to be perfect and special, with me not wanting you. I didn't trust myself to not fall into you, and then we would have still been in the cell and caught in our escape."

"We aren't running anymore," her eyes don't leave mine as her tongue darts out to lick her bottom lip. Oh, how I want to bite that lip. "Will you teach me, Ika?"

I feel my knees go weak; she really is as innocent as she appeared. I shift, so I am kneeling in front of her, and cup her face with both my hands.

"Stop me if you don't like it, Darlin'. I don't want to do anything you don't want me to." She nods and our noses brush against each other as I lower my face to hers.

Our lips met, and as her soft lips brush against mine, I feel more alive than ever before. Not trusting myself to overwhelm her body with kisses, I keep it short, kissing her fully on the mouth before pulling away. A soft growl escapes Trudy, her hand snaking up into my hair, slamming my face back to hers.

Chapter Twenty-Three

PRINCESS GERTRUDE

I slam his mouth to mine. His kiss was soft and sweet, but there wasn't enough of it. I relish in the feel of his beard brushing against my face. I kiss his upper lip, then lower lip, darting my tongue out to lick against his lips. His mouth parts and I snake my tongue inside. I had never kissed anyone before and wasn't sure if I was doing it properly. All I know was I cannot stop; I need to keep kissing him as much as I need to breathe.

Letting my want drive me, I continue kissing Ika. My hands combing through his soft silky hair, I move so I am kneeling with him. Ika's arms wrap around my waist, anchoring our bodies together. His hand slides down until it is squeezing my butt cheek. I can feel his hard length pressed against my stomach, as he uses his grip to grind me lightly against him. Ika is the one to break the kiss, pulling his head back to look me in the eyes.

"We need to stop, Darlin'."

"Why?" I pant, out of breath from our kissing, my face flushed with pleasure.

"Believe me Darlin', I want to keep going. But if we keep

kissing, something is going to happen, and I don't want your first time to be on a forest floor."

"What about what I want, Ika?"

"And what is it you want?" he growls; eyes still bright with his desire.

I know I can be myself and trust Ika with everything. So, taking a deep breath, I let the words fall out, my hands still running through his hair. The leather band that had been keeping it tied up had fallen out underneath my roaming fingers, and it is all loose and free for me to enjoy now.

"You, Ika. I want you."

At my declaration, Ika's lips crash back to mine, while pushing me back gently. Without breaking the kiss, and with some awkward manoeuvring of my legs, I end up laying down on my bedroll with Ika half on top of me.

Ika's hands roam up from my waist to my face, cupping it gently while he pulls back to look at me again.

"What do you want, Darlin'?" His voice husky with desire.

"I want to feel good, Ika. I want you to make me feel good, for us both to." Desire lacing my voice.

He growls again, and I chuckle lightly. Leaning down to brush his lips against my ear, he whispers, "Darlin', I will make you feel the best you've ever felt." Grazing his teeth against my earlobe, he places a small kiss behind my ear, before kissing gently down my neck. I sigh in pleasure. No one has ever touched me like this, but after Ika, no one else ever would.

"Only you, Ika." I whisper. He looks up, his sea green eyes meeting my gaze from where he is currently kissing my neck. "I am yours Ika, only yours, eternally yours."

If possible, his eyes heat even more at my words. He continues kissing down my neck, trailing down to the top of my jacket. His hands came up to the buttons as he kneels over me, pausing he looks back at me.

"You're sure, Darlin'?" I nod, filled with nerves and anticipation, not trusting myself to speak. "Stop me anytime, okay?" I smile and nod again.

His fingers made quick work of my buttons, undoing them until my jacket hangs open, and he can see my white camisole. My breasts heave with my laboured breathing. Ika resumes kissing my neck, moving down to skim his nose across my collar bone, and placing a kiss at the hollow of my throat. He groans as his hands cup both my breasts. I am not small, but not large, either. As I was unable to ride with a corset, I had not been wearing one when I left the Palace. I only had the built-in shelf bra on the camisole. That, combined with the tight fit of the riding jacket and my average size, allowed me to be secure while riding.

I felt Ika grow harder against my leg, as he pinches my nipples through my camisole. I shift slightly, and Ika sat back on his heels, taking the time to look down and admire me. I use the absence of his body to sit up and remove my jacket, meeting Ika's eyes as I pull the camisole over my head. Bare to the waist, Ika's gaze does not leave mine. He keeps looking me in the eye, leaning back into me as he takes my mouth in another passionate kiss. Ika presses me back down into the bedroll, positioning himself to lie directly on top of me this time. I shift my legs under my skirt, giving him space to lie between them.

We moan in unison as we feel his cock press against my centre. Even through all our clothing I can feel his throbbing hardness as his hips grind into me. Using one arm to keep his weight off me, Ika's other hand reaches between us to fondle my breast. I cannot stop the sounds of ecstasy leave my mouth, the feel of his calloused palm rubbing against my sensitive skin and peaked nipple it's almost too much for me to handle. Needing more, I reach my hands down, pulling my skirt up to sit around my waist, minimising the clothing between us. Ika moans in pleasure as his restrained cock rubs against my white satin panties. Shifting back to his knees, he looks down at the wetness visible through the fabric. His hands move to my inner thighs, thumbs brushing at the edge of my panties.

"You okay with this Darlin'?" His heated voice is filled with both his kindness and desire.

I nod. "I need you, Ika. Please?"

I can see his cock pulse against his pants at my words.

"I'm still not gonna fuck you for the first time on the forest floor," my heart soars at the same time my stomach sinks at his words. Before I have a chance to respond, Ika continues "but I'll make you feel good, Darlin'."

His hands continue their roaming, running up and down my thighs, tormenting me.

"Please, Ika?" I beg my desperation clear, eyes closing in anticipation. I am not sure how much more of this sweet torture I can take.

I feel his hands run up my outer legs. When he reaches my panties, he slips his fingers to hook under the fabric, pulling it with him as he brushed down my legs. I hear his breath catch as my pussy is bared to him. I open my eyes to find him holding my panties in one hand, making eye contact with me, he inhales deeply before his eyes close on a groan.

I grow wetter thinking about what the scent of me on my panties could be doing to him. His eyes spring open, and I can see his hunger for me flash in his eyes. Dropping my panties from his face, he leans forward and kisses the top of my pubic bone. He slowly moves his kisses down over my mound until he meets my pussy lips. Inhaling my scent again, he blows directly onto my clit, causing me to shiver in delight. Then his warm breath is replaced with his hot wet mouth, sucking on my clit. Needing something to hold on to, I reach down and twine my hands in his hair, simultaneously holding it off his face and holding his face to my pussy. I can feel his tongue dart out and circle my clit before licking up and down my slit.

Looking down our eyes meet, watching each other as he

devours my pussy. My walls contract and I feel so empty clenching around nothing.

"More, please." I moan out.

Tingles brake out across my body as his hand skims up my inner thigh, before meeting his lips at my core. He moans into me, the vibration drawing my centre tighter. I am going to explode with pleasure. Swiping his finger though my wetness, he begins circling my tight hole.

"Ohhhh, I-Ika!" I exclaim, "That's so intense. Ah, I'm so close!"

His finger slips into me, and I pulse at his entrance, my pussy trying to suck him deeper into me.

"Oh fuck! You are so tight, Darlin'. Does this greedy little pussy feel good, Darlin'? Do you like feeling me in you?"

"Ikaaaaaa, I'm... I'm gonna..." I say through my moans.

My hips shift as I pull his head back to my pussy. The second his lips kiss my clit I shatter. My whole-body quakes, my back arches and heat spreads from my centre as I explode on his face and finger. Ika continues kissing, licking and stroking me until I sag back to the bedroll, coming down from my high. Ika crawls over me, kissing me senseless, allowing me to taste myself. I break the kiss and pull back to meet his gaze.

"Did you like cummin' on my face, Darlin'?"

His dirty words make me blush, even after what we just did, "Yes, Ika, you make me feel better than I have ever felt, than I have ever been able to make myself feel."

He lets out a small grunt and hangs his head, leaning against my chest. "You are gonna be the death of me, woman."

"Can I touch you now? Can you teach me how to make you feel that good?" I don't give him the chance to respond, reaching my hand down, cupping his cock through his pants. I move my hand, rubbing up and down his long shaft. He moans as his hips instinctively buck into my hand.

Ika lifts his hand, and begins kissing one breast while massaging the other, while his cock continues to grind into my hand. Brazenly I slide my other hand up under his shirt and run my fingers over his hard-defined muscles, dipping down to undo his pants.

Ika bucks as my fingertips meet his bare cock. I wrap both of my hands around the soft velvety skin and squeezed him gently.

"What you do want, Ika?" I ask, repeating his earlier words back to him.

"I want you to make me feel good, Darlin'." He murmurs against my breast, echoing me.

"Teach me, Ika. Tell me what to do."

"Tighten your grip a little, Darlin'. Mmm. Yes, like that. Now move your hands up and down my cock." I stroke his cock, feeling his heart beating pulse against my palm. I swipe my hand up and press my thumb into the flatness under his head, swiping my thumb across the pre-cum that had started to seep out of his cock. Leaving one hand rubbing his cock, Ika watches as I pull his pre-cum up to my mouth and lick it off my thumb. The moment it hits my lips, his cock explodes, his cum covering my hands.

Chapter Twenty-Four

PRINCESS GERTRUDE

*R*emoving his shirt, Ika wipes his cum off both himself and me.

"Come on, Darlin', we should probably go and clean up."

Ika stands tucking himself back into his pants. He looks down at me, still sprawled on the floor mostly naked, and groans.

"Darlin', you are so breathtaking."

Ika leans down to help me stand, and I begin putting my clothing to rights.

"Don't worry too much, Darlin', it's all gonna come off again when we get to the stream."

Once my clothing was somewhat covering my body, I take Ika's hand, and we walk down to the stream. It is still very dark, but I can see the world starting to brighten with the sun over the horizon. As we get to the rock bed, Ika stops and faces me. Still shirtless, my hands drift up to lay on his bare chest, lightly playing with his chest hair. Ika kisses my nose, my cheeks and my mouth. His kiss is possessive and filled with tender care.

Ika's hands rise to my shoulders, and he pushes off my jacket. My hands falling to my sides so the jacket can drop to the floor. Ika's hands find my waist, lifting my camisole over my head, leaving me bare to the waist again. Before Ika kept undressing me, I reach down and undo his pants. He allows them to fall to the ground while stepping out of his boots. Naked, Ika's attention returns back to me. I turn around showing him how to undo my skirt, holding my hand to allow me to step out of them. Ika leans down and skims my panties down and over my boots, kneeling to remove my boots and stockings.

Standing naked in the open is a new experience for me. I feel like I should be self-conscious, or cautious of who could be watching, and yet instead I felt safe. I always feel safe and whole in Ika's presence. Ika leads me into the stream. I did not notice that Ika had grabbed the soap bar until he was lathering me up within the shallow water. We don't speak as we gently wash and caress each other, showing our emotions through physical touch. Ika sits down in the water and I wash, and finger brush his hair. I love his hair. I do not think a day would go by where I will not want to touch it, to run my fingers through his hair and feel it tickle my palm.

Washed and clean again, we sit on the same rocks I had sat on yesterday morning. I am still processing everything that has happened in the last forty-eight hours. So much has happened, my life has changed completely. Sitting on the rocks with Ika, I feel a peace settle over me. Ika is my home. I watch as Ika braid his hair, and then enjoy the feeling of him braiding mine. Once we have air dried enough, we help each other dress, and make our way back to the campground.

"Get some sleep, Darlin'. We will leave in a few hours."

"Will you lay with me, Ika?" He grins and nods at me, pulling our bedrolls to be next to each other and lay down cuddling into Ika's side.

* * *

The sound of hooves trampling through the forest wakes us both. The sky is bright with the morning sun, and I think we have been asleep for a few hours. Ika jumps to his feet.

"Is that the King's Guard?" He whispers to me.

"It can't be, can it? Not so soon!" I whisper back. Whether it is the King's Guard or someone else, we don't need to alert them to our location. I had been so caught up in Ika, his touch and his body, I forgot that we are escaping from the Palace and that Harrison will be after us.

Scrambling, we collect all our possessions and quickly shove them into Stormy's saddlebags. I untie Stormy and begin leading her away from the clearing and the sounds of hooves that woke us up. As I have concealed us in the bushes, I hear two men enter our clearing.

"This campsite looks fresh," a deep gruff voice spoke.

"The fire isn't though. It's about a day old," replied a strained voice. Making me glad we hadn't bothered to light a fire this time.

"It could have been where they stayed on their way to the Palace."

"Well that's not much use to us, is it? We need to know where they have gone now, not where they were yesterday."

I look over at Ika, who is crouched behind a tree, trying to keep his large frame from being seen through the dense bushes. I can tell Ika was cursing himself for not being more alert to our surroundings, thinking that this could have been avoided if we left earlier or continued last night.

"The forest is littered with guards, Ika, what are we going to do?" I whisper to Ika, aware that we are not far from the clearing the guards are still in.

"I don't know, Darlin'. Have you got any ideas?"

The two guards start to walk back in the direction they had entered the clearing from.

"We have to lose them before we go home," I watch Ika's face light up with a giant grin at the word 'home', realising it is the first time I have called his place home. "We can't lead them there, but we can lead them somewhere else!"

I bend down and, gathering my skirts in my hands, I begin ripping pieces off.

"What are you doing?"

"We need to leave a trail. Do you know how to get to the Silent Wood from here?"

"You want to escape into the Silent Wood?"

"No! I want to lead them to the wood, so they get trapped! Keep up."

Ika's gaze appraises me like he had never seen me before.

"Okay, Darlin'."

Ika helps me up onto Stormy. It is much easier now my skirt has been ripped up to my thighs. Ika positions himself behind me on Stormy and takes the reins.

"I'll steer her, you can start your trail."

Walking at a slow pace, I lean over Ika's arm, placing pieces of my skirts on bushes and branches. Letting a few pieces fall to the ground behind us. It is a shorter walk than I thought it would be to arrive at the edge of the Silent Wood. We dismount from Stormy, and Ika shows me the point in the bushes where the Silent Wood begins. Not wanting to risk getting too close to the forest, I began scrunching up pieces and throwing them into the branches. Happy there were enough pieces within the Silent Wood to lure the guards in, I let Ika lead me to hide a few metres away from our trail to wait for the guards.

"I found something!" A guard calls out. He must have found my trail.

A second guard replies, "It leads that way! Quickly, men!"

The forest is suddenly full of the sounds of horses neighing, hooves trampling and men shouting as they run to follow the trail.

We sink further into our crouch as we hear the men approach. Not wanting to draw their attention away from the trail, I hold my breath, not even daring to whisper to Ika. I watch in shock as ten guards run past us and into the Silent Wood without hesitating or checking their surroundings.

As they disappear from sight, Ika picks me up and swings me around.

"You are amazing, Darlin'." I blush and kiss him passionately on his mouth, losing myself within his kiss. Ika breaks the kiss first, leaning back to look at me as he places my feet back on the ground.

"We should get home, Darlin', before any other guards come looking for us."

"Okay Ika, take me home."

We mount back up on Stormy, and Ika wraps his arms around my waist as he takes the reins again. I place my hands on his forearms, lightly playing with the hair there. Ika leans in to kiss me on the side of my neck as he looks over my shoulder and starts Stormy off galloping. My mind spins with thoughts about the guard's arrival. Would Harrison really be hunting us down for the rest of our lives? Was it fair to ask Ika to go through all of that for me?

Chapter Twenty-Five

IKA

*H*aving my Darlin' Trudy pressed against me has to be the best feeling in the world. The curves of her body fit perfectly against me as we ride Stormy home. I feel Trudy sigh out a deep breath.

"Is something wrong, Darlin'?"

"Harrison isn't going to stop, Ika. He will be after us forever. Are you sure you want to deal with that, just for me?"

"Trudy, Darlin', I know we haven't known each other long. Fuck we barely know each other at all. But my soul knows you, reaches for you. I am sure with every cell in my body that I am yours, and if that means dealing with your crazy brother, then that is what we will do. Together."

Trudy tilts her head back and looked up at me.

"How did I get to be so lucky? What did I do to deserve to find you?"

"I think you got that the other way around, Darlin'. I'm not sure what I did to deserve showing up on my doorstep."

Stormy enters the clearing where my pride and joy is held. I had built this cabin with my father just after we left the Palace. It took us a good while to get everything to my mother's wishes, but it was our first real family home.

It looks like a standard log cabin in the woods, and while it was a log cabin it is far from standard. The house stretches out to hold four large bedrooms, a living, dining and sitting room, kitchen and outdoor shaded area.

"Welcome home, Darlin'."

Trudy lets out a sigh, smile spreading out across her face. "Home."

KING HARRISON

"What do you mean, the guards haven't returned?" I question Joseph, the captain of my guard. He is a stocky man, roughly the same height as me, with skin tanned from years in the sun, and pale blonde hair. His blue eyes shine, brightening his face.

"There have been no reports of the men since they entered the woods yesterday, Your Majesty." Joseph reports back in a short and clipped manner.

"Any word or sighting of my sister?" I continue.

As Joseph opens his mouth to speak, Evalyn emerges from behind a pillar, "Your sister, Your Majesty? Is that what all this fuss is over? Don't tell me you have actually found her?"

This is the last thing I wanted, and thankfully Joseph knows that.

"No ma'am," Joseph replies, "Just a standard patrol. We had a prisoner who was a person of interest. We believed he might know of Princess Gertrude's where-abouts, but he has escaped in the night."

"I did not ask you; you fool. I asked the King." Her fury at Joseph speaking for me evident in her voice, she turns back to me. "You suspect you are able to find her?"

"I don't know, Evalyn. What Joseph has just told you is the truth. We currently do not know where she is, we haven't known for four years now."

That ungrateful bitch, she had everything, and she has runaway *twice*? She is a Princess, had everything at her fingertips, and even had the chance to marry *Him*, and she turns it all way for a peasant? I *will* get to the bottom of this.

THE STORY CONTINUES IN:

The King and The Prince
Kingdom of Daes Duo: Book 2
A forbidden royal romance.

ACKNOWLEDGMENTS

Thank you to my tribe of people. Without your guidance, love and support – I really would not have gotten here!

Firstly, a huge thank you to my partner in all things, my Hayden. You supported me when I didn't support myself, thank you for being my person, for allowing me to bounce ideas off you and not calling me crazy.

Thanks to Isabou, Bec and Donagh, for being there when I couldn't think, and beta reading for me.

A huge thank you to my girl, Jess, for being excited for me, challenging me and editing for me.

For Katrina, Aleks, Lukazs, Tiarne, Hoff, Jean, Sonia and countless others, thank you for always cheering me on and encouraging me.

And last, but not at all least, thank you to my parents. Adele, Martin and Treena, I would not be the dreamer that I am without you all.

ABOUT THE AUTHOR

Heidi grew up in south-west Sydney, Australia, and now lives in the Southern Highlands of NSW with her marvellous boyfriend, Hayden. Heidi is a dog mum to two beautiful, attention loving girls, Amber and Daisy. She is 24 and has 2 brothers and a sister.

Heidi had difficulties learning and maintaining the standard literacy and numeracy requirements in school, until she found her love for reading. It all started with a cringe worthy obsession over a certain Edward Cullen, which has fuelled Heidi to go on to reading 200+ books a year.

With a passion for reading, Heidi began writing short stories, and has always had an overactive imagination. Heidi comes across as a loud, boisterous person, who is actually a shy girl terrified of rejection. This fear held Heidi captive for a long time and prevented Heidi from sharing any of her work - until now.

"Bite the bullet" is a term often used in Heidi's family. Heidi is now taking that step out of her comfort zone, and self-publishing her first complete book - The Princess and The Lumberjack. Heidi hopes you enjoy! Please leave any feedback or reviews for Heidi, as that is how authors are better able to reach their readers.

FOLLOW ME!

Want to keep up with all the new releases from H. L. Muller?
Make sure you sign up for her newsletter for all the latest on upcoming books:
www.hlmullerauthor.com

Or you can check out her social media:
www.instragram.com/heidilmuller
www.facebook.com/hlmuller.author
www.goodreads.com/author/show/20148777.H_L_Muller